North Ayrshire Libraries

This book is to be returned on or before
the last date stamped below.

D1513508

CANCELLED

**MOST ITEMS CAN BE RENEWED BY TELEPHONE
OR ONLINE AT http://prism.talis.com/north-ayrshire/**

For those who love and seek to understand horses . . . and the horsemen who care, and share their knowledge.

* * *

Thanks to my family and friends who have supported me during the writing of this book and a special thanks to my cover model Tessa Silcock.

I'd also like to thank Carol Martin for the use of her beautiful stallion Ataahua Valentino.

Thanks to my editor Francie Wafer, and to Vicki Marsdon, Emma Beckett and the team at Penguin for inviting me to write this series.

I am eternally grateful to my friend and namesake Trudy Nicholson for her constant communication from the other side of the world while drawing the images for this book.

And most importantly thanks to the horsemen and horses who have got me this far . . .

Summer
with
Horses

by Trudy Nicholson

PUFFIN BOOKS

PUFFIN BOOKS
Published by the Penguin Group
Penguin Group (NZ), 67 Apollo Drive, Rosedale
North Shore 0632, New Zealand (a division of Pearson New Zealand Ltd)
Penguin Group (USA) Inc., 375 Hudson Street
New York, New York 10014, USA
Penguin Group (Canada), 90 Eglinton Avenue East, Suite 700, Toronto
Ontario, M4P 2Y3, Canada (a division of Pearson Penguin Canada Inc.)
Penguin Books Ltd, 80 Strand, London, WC2R 0RL, England
Penguin Ireland, 25 St Stephen's Green
Dublin 2, Ireland (a division of Penguin Books Ltd)
Penguin Group (Australia), 250 Camberwell Road, Camberwell
Victoria 3124, Australia (a division of Pearson Australia Group Pty Ltd)
Penguin Books India Pvt Ltd, 11, Community Centre
Panchsheel Park, New Delhi – 110 017, India
Penguin Books (South Africa) (Pty) Ltd, 24 Sturdee Avenue
Rosebank, Johannesburg 2196, South Africa

Penguin Books Ltd, Registered Offices: 80 Strand, London, WC2R 0RL, England

First published in Puffin Books, 2009
1 3 5 7 9 10 8 6 4 2

Copyright © Trudy Nicholson, 2009

The right of Trudy Nicholson to be identified as the author of this work in terms of
section 96 of the Copyright Act 1994 is hereby asserted.

Front cover photographs by Trudy Nicholson
www.nicholsonphotography.co.nz
Back cover photograph © iStockphoto.com
Illustrations by Trudy A. Nicholson

Designed and typeset by Pindar NZ
Printed in Australia by McPherson's Printing Group

ISBN 978 0 14330459 3
A catalogue record for this book is available
from the National Library of New Zealand.

www.penguin.co.nz

Contents

PART 1

Horses at the Beach

Horse Heaven

The old hut, standing a hundred metres from the beach among the tussock grass, driftwood and sandhills, was the girls' home for the summer holidays. Suzy, Alexa and Lucy were best friends, and they had this part of the world all to themselves. They had all they needed – no shopping malls or movie theatres, just each other and their horses: Ripple, Liquorice and Hope. The girls lived, breathed and now dreamed horses.

The hut was pretty basic – the door was a rickety structure that hung on a slight angle on rusted and worn hinges – but they didn't mind. Following one of their many fireside conversations they had named it 'Horse Heaven', and agreed that this was the best place on earth. 'In fact, this must be heaven on earth,' Suzy had remarked. They had even found a flat piece of driftwood and made a sign for the old hut, and Lucy had nailed it to the rough timber boards at the front entrance.

'I declare this here mansion be named "Horse Heaven", to be known from now on as "HH",' she announced as she pulled off the saddle blanket that had been covering the sign. Driftwood served many purposes around HH, from building pens and providing firewood to decorating the grounds. The girls enjoyed being creative around the hut when the horses needed a rest. They had formed a path to the door and edged it with driftwood and shells, and a horse sculpture was being created out the front to give the place a unique horse-ranch feel.

It could get cold in the hut at night, so the girls wrapped themselves up in their sleeping bags and used the horses' extra rugs as quilts. Hay covered in old sacking made soft, spongy beds and provided extra warmth. Things were much more civilised in HH than when they were 'roughing it' in their tent at White Cloud Station, where their horses had come from. They even changed into their pyjamas at night – in the girls' eyes the hut was as palatial as the Hilton Hotel.

Besides, if the weather turned really bad they could always go back to the beach house where Lucy's folks were staying, although this wasn't really part of their plan. They enjoyed their time together too much to return to the relative luxury of the beach house. They relished the freedom of fending for themselves, and not having to worry about adult ears listening in on their conversations. This was their special time together with their horses – doing things their way – and having adults around might put a damper on things. Their energy bounced off one another, and their secrets and horse talk were for them and them alone while they were in HH.

* * *

After a long, exhilarating day's riding on the beach and beyond the girls were weary, and they had settled down early in their sleeping bags. The evening was still, and the full moon shone through the broken window of the hut onto their faces as they drifted off to sleep. The three horses were munching happily on piles of hay, in the yards the girls had put together out of driftwood and timber scraps.

Suddenly the peace was shattered as Alexa erupted into fits of laughter.

'Control that horse of yours, Suzy,' she spluttered.

'At least tell him to turn the volume down – he's farting like a carthorse. I thought that green grass in the swamp paddock would gas him up and have this effect.'

Suzy and Lucy sat upright in their sleeping bags and joined in her laughter.

'Typical bloke!' shrieked Alexa, who had two younger brothers.

Suzy leaned forward and peeped out the window. 'That's not my horse making those rude noises – it's yours, Alexa! And Ripple says you'd better take back that chauvinistic re-mark too!'

Any noise seemed to echo round this part of the beach, which had a tall cliff-face at the northern end and hills behind. Whatever the mechanics of it, Liquorice was putting the power of echo to the test that night. The girls couldn't stop laughing, and they were all wide awake again.

'That's it! I give up trying to sleep – anyone for hot chocolate?' Suzy wrapped her 'quilt' around her shoulders and waddled toward the thermos she had filled earlier, trying not to trip over the edge of the rug. Lucy and Alexa sat up in their beds while Suzy made them hot chocolate and grabbed a packet of biscuits from the old tea-chest that served as their pantry.

'So what's happening tomorrow, you two?' she said as she stirred the hot chocolate.

'Swimming with the horses?' Lucy suggested, perched up in her bed as if she was waiting for room service.

'Beach racing!' Alexa put in.

Suzy passed them their drinks, then she sat down on the doorstep and sipped at her own.

'The stars are so clear, and there's an amazing reflection of the moon across the water. Wow, it's like daylight – hey, anyone for a moonlight ride?'

'Let's go for it!' Alexa shrieked, jumping out of bed.

They quickly finished their drinks, then they

bridled their horses and headed down the path toward the moonlit beach. 'Where else in the world could you ride in your pyjamas?' Alexa snorted. 'We have this whole beach to ourselves! Yay, I'm off – see ya!'

Hope shied at the white breakers and 'floating things' that sometimes drifted against her legs. 'C'mon, girl,' Lucy laughed as the horse splashed, trying to free a piece of debris that was clinging to her leg. 'It's just seaweed!

'Oh, you're a silly girl!' she muttered as she rebalanced herself after slipping sideways. 'It's not a horse-eating crocodile, you know!'

But Hope wasn't convinced, and kept spooking and snorting.

Suzy laughed from the safety of the beach. 'Hey be careful, she might dump you in the water!'

True to form, Alexa and Liquorice were already cantering down the beach, clearly visible in the bright moonlight.

Ripple pricked his ears and stepped out with a long stride beside the water, where the silver reflection of the moon rippled over it. He seemed to be enjoying his trek. Catching sight of Liquorice galloping back, he stopped and stood with his neck high, watching and waiting for them to get closer. Suzy gazed up at the bright stars above, and her friend Mike's words popped into her mind: 'You can do anything you want, Suzy. You and Ripple can reach the stars if you want; you can make dreams come true.'

Suzy smiled, threw the reins on Ripple's wither, lifted her arms above her head and reached as far as she could towards the sky.

'*This* dream *is* true. Thanks, Mike, for giving me such an awesome horse!' Then she leant down toward Ripple's neck. 'This is horse heaven,' she whispered.

2

Sam

The girls were up early the next morning as they wanted to catch low tide so they would have plenty of room on the beach to gallop. The sand was so much smoother when it was wet, and it also meant they could keep clear of the deeper sand and driftwood higher up the beach where the horses risked pulling a tendon or tripping.

'Maybe we should put the saddles on the horses today,' Suzy said as she walked back into HH to get her tack.

'Good thinking!' replied Alexa. 'It'll give us a bit more grip, especially as we want to have a blat! Besides, Liquorice can become quite excitable when the heat increases so I need all the grip I can get!

'Maybe we should get into our clothes too,' she laughed. 'Sticky-bum jods, in fact! Anything to help hold me on!'

Ripple was already tied up at the back of the hut, where Suzy had been grooming him. She liked him to be spotless and knew that grooming was good for toning him. She admired her horse when he pricked his ears and looked at her with both eyes while she rustled around sorting out the gear. Mike had told her it was good when a horse 'gives you both eyes'. She knew Ripple was focused and attentive.

'What a handsome boy you are,' she whispered to

him quietly. 'Just the most handsome horse in the world. In fact, I'd go so far as to say you have a distinguished look about you, and you certainly have an intelligent look – you're a true gentleman. Mike did such a good job of starting you.'

At that her thoughts were suddenly elsewhere, and she wondered how Mike was doing at Marble Arch Ranch. It must be so exciting to work with horses on that level, and to be able to 'read' them the way he does . . . one day, she thought . . . then her daydream came to an abrupt end and she was back to reality, beside Ripple who was pulling at her sweatshirt, playing, as if to get her attention. Nearby the other girls were saddling up their horses, and Suzy put Ripple's saddlecloth on him, pulling it back to flatten the hair underneath. Next she placed her general-purpose saddle on top of the cloth. As she reached under his stomach for the girth Ripple suddenly lurched sideways, alarmed, yet careful to avoid Suzy.

'What is it, boy? What are you sensing that I can't?'

Ripple's ears were pricked in the direction of the bushes behind them. He gave a high-pitched honk and his body turned as far as the rope would allow. His neck went rigid and his body trembled as he snorted again. In an instant Hope and Liquorice had picked up on the warning and were looking in the same direction, heads high, nostrils flared and ears pricked.

'D'you think it's one of those wild pigs Dad told us about?' Lucy asked. 'He said to keep an eye out for them.'

'Damned if I know, but something sure is setting them off,' Alexa replied as she mounted Liquorice. 'I'll take Liqui over and see what it is.'

She gave Liquorice a squeeze with her legs and the mare moved in the direction of the rustling bush. Suddenly the horse stopped and refused to take another step, arching her neck and pricking her ears in the direction of the bush. She pranced when Alexa urged her on, and Alexa knew not to pressure her horse too much or she would rear.

Alexa could just make out a shape in the bush, and the sun glinted off what looked like a pair of eyes . . .

'Holy hell, it's a beast!' she shrieked.

She was just about to turn her horse when a boy stood up and walked out of the bush. At this Liquorice sighed and lowered her head, realising it was a human being.

'You frightened the life out of my horse!' Alexa yelled. 'What are you playing at, rustling around in the bushes – what's your name, kid?'

'Sam,' the boy replied, looking petrified at the sight of the raging girl above him. 'Sorry about frightening your horse . . . I was only . . .'

'Yeah, well, like – think about it, eh!'

'I only wanted to give the horses these.' The boy held out his hands, which were full of neatly sliced pieces of carrot. Liquorice leaned toward his open hands and took one of the pieces.

'Ahh, no wonder Liquorice doesn't mind you. So, where do you live, and how did you know the horses were here anyhow?' Alexa was still looking fierce, and the boy anxiously tried to answer her questions.

'Up there.' He pointed to a hill to the west. 'I come and stay here with my uncle and aunt in the holidays. That's their farm, but there aren't any horses. I'm at boarding school now, so I can only come here in the school holidays.'

'You don't look old enough for boarding school,' Alexa exclaimed, rubbing Liquorice on the neck.

'I'm at prep school – I'm 11,' the boy answered.

'Well, not much of a farm if they don't have horses, huh?' said Suzy, who was now holding a calmer Ripple. 'Would you like to give Ripple a piece of carrot too?'

'Hi, Ripple; I'm Sam,' the boy mumbled as he walked toward Ripple, who poked his nose out toward him.

'You like horses then, do you Sam?' Suzy asked. 'Do you ride?'

'Yeah, sometimes I go to the riding school in West

15

Grove, in the weekends. Other than that I don't get much of a chance. We used to have a horse here but it died.'

He lowered his head and looked away.

'So how'd you like a ride on Ripple?' The boy looked up quickly, a huge grin on his face. He had an amazing smile and his whole face lit up so much that he didn't have to speak.

'Suzy!' Alexa frowned. 'You can't let a stranger ride your horse!'

Alexa had a habit of being an authority on everything, but Suzy was used to this and ignored her. She had a gut feeling about her horse and Sam. She took the stirrup leathers up four holes.

'Come here, Sam, I'll give you a leg up. You can ride him to the cave over there and back, but only at a walk – okay?'

Suzy liked the way Sam held the reins loosely, without pulling on Ripple's mouth, and she noticed how the horse sensed which direction to turn in by a slight movement of the boy's shoulders. Sam was quite a natural on the back of the horse. Ripple wandered back like the good horse he was and came to a halt the instant Sam sat more upright.

'Thanks, Ripple,' Sam murmured as he leant forward, encouraging Ripple to turn his head back toward his hand for a piece of carrot. Ripple crunched on the carrot as Sam swung his leg over and landed on the ground.

'Cool. Thanks. He's an awesome horse. I'd love to have a horse like him!'

Suzy adjusted the leathers and mounted Ripple as Sam walked away with his hands in his empty pockets, glancing back once or twice as he headed towards the farmhouse that was just visible in the distance.

'C'mon, race ya!' Alexa yelled, giving Liquorice a firm nudge in the sides. 'Last one to Devil's Cave has to cook tonight!'

At that Suzy gathered up the reins, leant forward in the saddle and squeezed her legs into Ripple's sides. He tossed his head as if to say 'Let's go', and in a few strides he was beside Hope and Liquorice. Side by side the horses galloped along the wet sand, which made a hollow noise as the thundering hooves pounded on it. At that speed the girls' eyes watered as the sea breeze hit their faces. It was hard to see clearly, but it didn't matter because they were at one with their horses – the thundering legs were an extension of their own bodies and the horses' eyes became theirs – it was so exhilarating as they galloped to the far end of the beach.

'Yay, we won!' Suzy shrieked as Ripple came down to a walk. He blew and took advantage of the long rein by stretching out his neck, then he tossed his head and looked around for the other horses.

Ripple could easily outrun Hope and Liquorice as he had a long, easy stride for his size. Lucy and Alexa shared the cooking that night while Suzy watched over the horses as they picked at the grass in the swamp paddock. The fences were a bit makeshift and they didn't want to risk any of the horses wandering away. While keeping one eye on the horses she made up the feeds for the next morning and put the filled hay-nets in the yards ready for the fast-approaching evening. The days seemed to go too fast at HH, she thought.

3

Ripple's Gone!

When they were not riding, the girls found plenty to fill in their days. HH became a work of art in itself, and after only one week the pathway leading to the door had been completed and paved with shells. Sam, passing by on his way fishing, noticed the horse sculpture taking shape and collected some driftwood so that he could add his own artistic touch. The sculpture was slowly becoming recognisable as a horse, which the girls affectionately named Bones.

All sorts of treasures, such as nets, bits of wreckage from boats, bottles and even a crayfish trap, were washed up onto the beach at high tide and left among the tussocks and driftwood when the water receded. When they weren't riding, rummaging through the treasures on the beach was a favourite pastime. Lucy had found an old, frayed rope and attached it to Bone's rump to form a tail. HH was adorned with some of their other finds, including the crayfish trap, which was hung on the front wall.

The whole place was magical and it was all theirs. Apart from Lucy's parents and Sam's occasional visits no one else came to their secret place. It was as if it was the only place on earth – and they were the only people.

* * *

'I'll go and give the horses their morning feeds,' Lucy said one morning, pulling on a sweatshirt over her pyjamas and wiping the sleep from her eyes. 'You lazybones can stay in bed for a while. The horses will need time to digest their food before we ride anyhow. I'll be back in a tick.'

She nudged the door open with her foot and stretched up to the sky as she stood on the step, admiring yet another glorious morning. The weather was supposed to get worse later, but even if it did rain it wouldn't matter, Lucy thought.

'I love the smell of sea air!' she enthused.

Suzy had prepared the hard feeds the night before, so Lucy added some water and walked around to the yards. When she got there she dropped the buckets in horror and ran back to the hut. Shoving open the door, she shrieked, 'Suzy, it's Ripple!'

'What? What about Ripple?' Suzy leapt out of bed and raced toward her.

'He's like . . . like . . . he's gone!'

'What do you mean "GONE"?' Alexa yelled, her expressive eyes big with shock. 'D'you mean . . . ?'

'No, not dead, gone. Like, gone gone! Like, not there gone! He's not in his yard gone! Like, missing gone!'

'I'm sure I put the rail up last night,' Suzy called as

she ran around the corner of the hut. 'He couldn't have pushed it down . . . besides, I know Ripple and he wouldn't stay away long, or go far, even if he had got himself out!'

'He's not here,' Alexa said, stating the obvious as she followed hard on Suzy's heels. 'Oh my gawd, someone's taken him. He's been stolen!'

'But there's no one around here who would or *could* steal him,' Lucy gasped.

'Mm, except for . . .' Alexa's voice tailed off.

'What d'you mean?' Suzy asked. 'Stop being so mysterious – it's no time for mind games.'

'Okay, okay – I reckon it's that "Sam I am" boy!' Alexa replied in typically impetuous Alexa fashion. 'He was pretty blimmin' keen on Ripple.

'That's it,' she said fiercely. 'I'm going up to that house on the hill, and when I find him I'll stretch his wingnuts right off the side of his head. Just shows – you do someone a favour and that's the thanks you get, eh? Like, we even let him help build Bones! Typical of a kid like that – sneaky little brat. He was probably planning it that other day . . .'

'Oh for goodness sake, shut up Alexa!' Suzy demanded furiously. 'We need to think clearly about what to do.'

Something inside told Suzy it couldn't be Sam – after all, she had been so kind to him – or could it be? Maybe Alexa was right? And if it wasn't Sam who was it, and where was Ripple?

Suddenly it all felt too much and she began to cry. The three friends huddled together, sniffling in harmony, distraught and stunned by Ripple's disappearance. They were soon interrupted by Hope's high-pitched neigh, followed by another.

'Listen to that echo,' Lucy said, turning her head to follow the sound, which seemed to come from two different directions.

'That's no echo!' exclaimed Alexa. 'That's coming from over by the cave.'

 'Cave! Oh my gawd, d'you think Ripple's over there, Suzy?' shrieked Lucy.

They raced toward the cave at the northern end of the beach.

'Ripple! Ripple!' Suzy yelled at the top of her lungs. There was a faint neigh from the direction of the cave. 'Why isn't he coming when I call him?' She peered desperately toward the cave. 'The tide's turning – he must be caught over there. If we don't get him out he'll get trapped and . . . and . . . he won't be able to come back.

'I'll have to climb around the edge of the rocks to the cave and get him,' Suzy said decisively, her panic forgotten. 'Quick, get me his halter and lead rope, Alexa.'

'But how will you get him back?' Lucy asked her. 'You can't walk him around the rocks – no horse could manoeuvre on those, they're too rough and unsteady.'

'I'll swim with him if I have to. Quickly, give me the halter,' she demanded as Alexa arrived back, breathing heavily. 'We haven't got time to waste!'

'Suzy, NO!' Alexa said. 'It's too dangerous! I don't want you to do this! Please don't!'

'What else can I do? D'you expect me to let my horse drown at full tide?'

Suzy ran toward the cave. The waves were now crashing in on the rocks, and before long the sea would have covered them. Suzy hung the halter and rope over her shoulder then, reaching up to a higher rock, she pulled herself up onto the rock-face. It was hard going – she had had no time to put on shoes, and the rocks cut into her bare feet. The sea was now splashing up and over her ankles, and she could hear it pounding in and around the blowhole. She knew she had to get past the rocks to reach the beach in front of the cave. She counted the waves, and noticed that every third one sprayed higher onto the rocks where she was heading. Timing her move carefully, she leaned into the side of the cliff and nervously stepped past the thundering sea below her. As she continued around towards the beach, which was not yet covered by the incoming tide, she caught a glimpse of Ripple. He was just in front of the entrance to the cave. He saw Suzy and gave a whinny.

Back on the first beach Lucy and Alexa watched anxiously.

'I'm not liking this one bit!' Lucy said, tears rolling down her cheeks as she tried to compose herself. 'I'm going to take Hope and go up to get my folks. We're going to need a rescue team! You stay here and keep an eye on things, and meet them when they arrive. Oh gawd, it's so remote out here – it'll take too long. I'm scared, Alexa, I'm really scared!'

'Me too,' Alexa said, her face white with fear. 'Just go! I'll be here.'

With no time to saddle up, Lucy quickly put on Hope's bridle, lined her up by the fence and hopped onto her bare back.

'C'mon, girl, we've got an important mission. We have to get help for Suzy and Ripple!'

She nudged the chestnut in her sides and they set off at a steady gallop toward her parents' holiday house. She knew they didn't have much time, and she just had to get there as quickly as she could.

4

Danger at the Cave

In less than an hour the tide would cover the rocks and the beach where Ripple was standing! Eventually the whole cave would fill with water, and echo the noise of the stormy tide! There would be no way to escape. The tide was rising so rapidly and the sea was becoming so rough that it seemed unlikely Suzy would be able to swim the horse back.

Suzy tried not to think about this, and kept focused on her trapeze act along the narrow rock-face. With a sense of relief she suddenly realised she was there – she had made it to the last rock – and she jumped down onto the sand below. The water engulfed her ankles as she paddled quickly toward her horse, who again whinnied, this time in a tone Suzy hadn't heard before.

'It's okay, Ripple, I'm here, I'm here now.' She swallowed her tears, hoping Ripple would not know how she was really feeling. She knew horses could pick up on emotions and body language, and she knew above all that Ripple would sense how she was feeling. She rubbed his neck and looked him over to check he was okay. The reason he hadn't come when she called was suddenly apparent – one of his legs was tangled up in an old fishing net that had a thick rope wrapped around a large log.

'Now I see why you couldn't come back – you're caught up in that old net! I'll get you out of that!' Suzy sighed with relief.

'Stand still, Ripple,' she said as she calmly checked his tangled leg. The sea was now reaching the spot where he was standing. 'You have to stand still so I can untangle the net. Remember how Mike taught you to stand quietly with ropes around your legs? Well, you have to do that for me now – there's nothing to be frightened of. Whoaaa! Stannnnd!' She didn't worry about putting on his halter, as it was obvious the horse couldn't move for now.

To her dismay Suzy noticed that the rope was wrapped tight around Ripple's fetlock. She desperately tried to untangle it but it wouldn't budge. She ran her hands back along the rope to the log, hoping she could untangle it at that end, but it had wound its way around the huge log and was embedded underneath it. There was no way she could free her horse!

The tiny butterflies she had felt at other times when she was nervous were babies compared to the giants that were now swarming inside her. As she felt the water surge up over her ankles a wave of panic engulfed her body. She was really frightened now. She knew about the fight, flight or freeze response horses experience when they are frightened. She also knew she couldn't flee and leave her beloved horse, but she quickly realised she couldn't fight the mighty rope that bound him. She felt frozen with fear.

Her mind was racing, but she could not think of a way for them to escape – she knew they were trapped. The relentless sea would wait for no one, and a terrible feeling of desperation washed over her. Tears of frustration, fear and helplessness began to trickle down her cheeks and she put her arms around Ripple's neck and sobbed into his curly mane.

'I think we're going to die here together,' she sobbed.

As if to agree, Ripple poked his nose forward and gently nuzzled into her chest. He closed his eyes as she hugged him tightly and sobbed some more.

Alexa was still watching anxiously from the beach. She could see that Suzy had reached Ripple, but the waves were crashing higher now and obscuring her view. As she stood helplessly, nervously chewing on her nails, she suddenly heard a voice behind her. She jumped and turned round, to see Sam holding onto a couple of snapper and his fishing gear.

'You girls better be careful,' he said, pointing to the clouds. 'Uncle George says there's a storm coming through. He says you'd better make sure you put good heavy rugs on your horses tonight. He says it could break up rough later, so make sure your horses are secure – you wouldn't want any of them escaping! I'm just heading back home now.'

'Great, just what I need, some more good news!' Alexa gasped. 'You're a bit late – we've already lost one.' She pointed to where Ripple and Suzy were just visible on the far beach. 'Suzy's going to swim Ripple back from the cave.'

'No way!' Sam exclaimed, his eyes as big as dinner plates. 'They'll drown if they try to swim back – the current's too rough along there, and they'll be trashed in the undercurrent towards the rock. They can't come back through the water! Uncle George has lived here all his life and he says you don't mess with the sea's fury!'

Suddenly he dropped his fish, rod and bag on the sand. 'I know – Castle Point!' he exclaimed, pointing to a rock on the cliff above. 'I know a way out! Wave to Suzy to stay where they are – they mustn't try and swim back, you hear me? They mustn't. I'll get to them!'

'Be careful, Sam, you're only a kid!' Alexa yelled after Sam as he ran through the tussocks and rocks toward the hill above the cliff-face.

She watched as the boy disappeared up the side of the steep hill and out of sight.

'Castle Point?'

5

Castle Point

Sam was gasping for breath by the time he reached the top of the cliff. Puffing, he made his way around the derelict castle, better known as the forbidden playground. He ran through the ruins, stumbling over the scattered debris, until he reached the entrance to a broad tunnel where stairs led down inside the hill. It had been boarded up some years back, but luckily the local kids had regularly used it as a hideaway – with a couple of hard kicks, and a few choice swear words picked up from his uncle, Sam managed to loosen the boards that covered the entrance. Pulling them off, he raced down the steps as fast as he could, grateful that there was just enough light for him to negotiate his way down inside the hillside.

He was familiar with the winding pattern of the steps because he had played there since he was very young, even though the area was supposedly 'out of bounds' to the children of his extended family. Even so, he still had to go carefully because the steps were very worn, and the edges crumbled as he bounded down them.

As he neared the bottom step where the tunnel opened out into the cave he called out to Suzy. He knew enough about horses to be aware that they could be alarmed by sudden noises, and he didn't want to panic Ripple.

26

He could see Suzy and Ripple silhouetted against the light outside, and he waded towards them. The water was splashing up onto the inside walls of the cave, and Sam knew they didn't have much time before they would be cut off from reaching the stairway that would take them back up.

'Suzy, Ripple – it's me – Sam,' he called. He could now see that already the water was around Suzy's thighs and touching Ripple's belly. 'Come this way,' he beckoned urgently. 'Come to me, quickly.'

'Sam!' Suzy's heart lurched as she made out the boy standing in the cave. 'I can't, Sam – Ripple's caught in a net! This leg's stuck. Sam, I'm so scared!'

Sam paddled toward them, saying calmly, 'You get that halter on and hold him steady. I'll check out what's happening here under the water.'

He stroked Ripple's shoulder and ran his hand down the horse's leg. He felt around under the water, then pulled out his fold-up fishing knife. Taking a huge breath, he filled his cheeks and dived under the water. To Suzy it seemed he was under the water forever. She talked gently to Ripple, keeping hold of his head collar rope while Sam splashed around with the net under the water. With one hand on Ripple's near fore, and his fishing knife in the other, he hacked at the stubborn rope.

'Be careful, Sam,' Suzy pleaded. 'Stannnnd, Ripple. Stand.'

Ripple stood still and Suzy could feel his tension as she stroked his neck. But he stood as told. Sam hacked at the thicker rope that was attached to the net, surfaced momentarily for air, then just as quickly dived under again. A few moments later he surfaced again, coughing and spluttering and gasping for air.

'You can tell him to walk on now,' he managed to say as he folded his fishing knife and put it back in the pouch on his belt. Ploughing through the deepening water, he pointed toward the steps. 'Follow me! There are stairs over here.'

Suzy began wading after him, with Ripple following.

'I hope you can swim!' Sam said, looking back at

them. 'There's one really deep bit here, and we'll have to swim through it to get to the steps. Ready?' Sam plunged into the water and began to swim towards the back of the cave.

'We can swim, can't we, Ripple,' Suzy replied, more to the horse than to Sam. 'Come on, Ripple – swim with me.'

It was a short but tough swim in the churning water, but they all reached the platform at the base of the steps in safety.

'Phew!' Suzy and Sam were both puffing, and Ripple's nostrils were flaring as he took rapid breaths. Elated that they had reached the platform in one piece, Sam announced the next stage of his rescue plan.

'I hope your horse can climb steps?'

'He hasn't done before!' Suzy answered. 'But he will! He trusts me and he'll follow.'

Sam led the way up the stairs, followed by Suzy, then Ripple following at the end of the lead rope. Ripple arched his neck for balance and followed Suzy as she and Sam climbed up the winding steps towards the light. He was a sure-footed horse – he had learnt to be from a young age up in the mountains at White Cloud Station. Some of the steps moved and gave way under his weight, but this didn't seem to alarm him – he understood he was to co-operate.

'We're there!' Sam announced as they reached the broken boards at the entrance to the tunnel. 'Yay! We made it!'

Exhausted, they sat among the ruins of the old castle and caught their breaths.

'It's not over yet, Suzy – we have to get down there before the storm sets in!'

Suzy looked down the side of the cliff and could just make out HH in the distance. It seemed an awfully long way down.

'Those black clouds are closing in; we'd better get going, Suzy,' Sam said, jumping up from the rock. 'I hope your horse doesn't mind climbing down some pretty steep hills!'

'No problem to Ripple,' Suzy said, 'eh, boy!'

* * *

Alexa, left by herself on the beach, had been straining her eyes to see them as she waited helplessly for time to pass. Finally seeing them in the distance, she mounted Liquorice and rode bareback to meet the bedraggled group as they reached the bottom of the hill.

She broke into a huge smile as she leapt from Liquorice's back and hugged Suzy, then Ripple.

'Hell, am I glad to see you guys! And as for you . . .' she said, grinning at Sam as she grabbed him by his ears and looked into his eyes. 'You're the most awesome kid alive, Sam! Awesome with a capital "A".' And at that she burst into tears.

'Jeez, I don't know why *I'm* crying,' she said, wiping her eyes. She could see that Sam was fading – he had virtually run a marathon in his mission to save Ripple and Suzy, and he was obviously feeling the effects now.

'Here, kid, I'll give you a leg up – you ride Liqui back to the hut.'

High on the back of the black horse, and quickly gaining his second wind, Sam rode like a conquering hero, a knight in shining armour returning from battle. He felt proud to be on the back of such a beautiful horse, and he rode on ahead of the girls as if to lead them back to safety. Liquorice pranced excitedly, as if she too felt triumphant and proud of the battle they had won.

Ripple walked between Alexa and Suzy, who had their arms draped over him. They were wet, cold and tired, and very relieved they were returning to the safety of HH with their new champion.

As they neared the hut they saw Joe's horse coach coming down Dusty Road. Alexa was relieved. 'Cool, Lucy obviously got to the beach house okay!'

'Yeah,' Suzy replied as it started to spit. 'Great timing!'

6

Sam's the Man

The horse truck pulled up just as they arrived back at HH. Serious rain was starting to fall, and thunder echoed around the valley, as if to announce the safe return of Ripple and Suzy. Liquorice joined in the celebration and reared, as if dancing on her hind legs in time with the thunder. Sam just leant forward and grinned, going with the movement, while secretly imagining for a moment he was part of a famous horse movie.

'See the way that kid sticks on when Liqui rears and prances?' Alexa said in amazement. 'If that were me I'd probably have fallen off! Damn good rider, that kid.'

Suzy smiled to herself. Is this the same kid whose ears she was going to wring off, she thought quietly. She laughed, knowing all too well how changeable and extreme Alexa could be. That's what she loved about her friend: under the tough exterior and often loud mouth was the softie who was her true friend. If the chips were down she knew she could rely on Alexa. Besides, she was never cruel to her own or anyone else's horses, and that was what really mattered in Suzy's eyes.

* * *

The coach was now parked and Lucy was pulling down the back ramp ready to load the horses. Her mother, Dawn, climbed out of the living area of the coach and ran toward the others. 'Thank goodness you're all safe!'

When Lucy had told them about Ripple and Suzy being stuck in the cave she had been desperately worried about what they would find when they arrived in the coach.

'Oh, thank God!' She waved to her husband, who was still behind the wheel, and called, 'Joe, they're all safe!'

She put an arm around Suzy. 'C'mon, you poor drenched souls, into the coach – we'll get some blankets around you. Joe will load the horses. Best we all head back up to the house until the storm passes over.'

Sam climbed down from Liquorice, and as Joe came towards him he handed Joe the lead rope and turned to walk away.

'Hey, you too, young man!' Dawn commanded. 'I've got some hot chocolate on for you as well.' She walked over to Sam and put one of Joe's large jackets around his shoulders. Sam climbed up the steps into the living area and looked around, amazed at how palatial it was inside. It was like a motel! He perched up beside Dawn, on a comfortable couch, while she prepared the hot drinks.

Lucy reached over Hope, who was already loaded on the coach, and pulled two waterproof horse rugs out of the nets above her head. She covered Ripple and Liquorice, then helped Joe load them onto the coach. They were well trained, and it was simply a matter of throwing their lead ropes over their necks and pointing them at the loading ramp. The rough weather didn't deter them either; they were well travelled and quite confident. Joe knew exactly how to drive a horse coach too – Lucy had instructed him often enough about 'how horses balance' while moving.

With the three horses loaded they all hopped on board and headed back up Dusty Road toward the holiday house. The wind was hitting the coach hard and Joe had the wipers on high speed. 'We're in for a rough night!' he said, taking a quick glance in the rear-view mirror. 'How are the wet ones doing back there? Are you all right, Sam? Warming up, I hope. We can telephone your Uncle George and Aunty Kate when we get back to the house.'

There was no answer – Sam was already fast asleep. Alexa leant over and pulled the blanket up over his shoulders.

* * *

'Sam, you'll have to stay over – the weather's set in and your uncle says it's fine with them if it's okay with you.' Dawn made this announcement as she threw another large log on the open fire. 'Not exactly the weather we had planned for our summer vacation, girls. Oh, and boys. Still, at least everyone's safe now, and the horses are settled in the barn for the night. Let's hope that Houdini Ripple doesn't make another escape tonight.' She laughed, trying to make light of the situation. 'What on earth would have made him go to that part of the beach in any case?'

'Goodness knows,' Suzy answered. 'I guess it's my fault. I couldn't have closed his gate rail properly. Maybe he pushed on it to reach some grass, or just scratched against it. He must have wandered out – he's a pretty inquisitive horse.

'Horses can sometimes become disorientated when they break free – maybe that happened and he got himself lost. The thing is – he would have come back if he hadn't got caught up in that terrible rubbishy net. It makes me so mad when beaches get littered; nets can be such a danger to sea life, and obviously horses. I'd say he's gone down and rolled in the soft sand by the cave, and that's when he got caught.'

'Yeah,' Lucy agreed, 'he's far too smart not to have returned otherwise. It's funny the way the other horses didn't call him earlier, though. Perhaps it was only when they sensed he was in danger that they started communicating out loud?'

'I guess we'll never really know – maybe they communicated with each other telepathically, and we simply didn't hear them,' Alexa suggested. 'And maybe it doesn't do to dwell on it too much. I hate to think what could have happened if Sam hadn't come by today!' She looked at Sam 'You're one awesome kid, "Sam I Am"! You're the man!'

They fell silent, each withdrawing into their own thoughts as they stared into the flames – each reliving the day's events, and thinking how grateful they were that Ripple and Suzy were safe.

Dawn, meanwhile, had left them and gone out to the kitchen. A little while later the pensive mood was broken when she walked in carrying a tray laden with four plates.

'Fish is on the menu tonight!' She smiled. 'Not only is this lad a hero, and obviously a talented horseman, but he's a great fisherman too!'

They laughed as they each reached for a plate, suddenly realising how hungry they were.

'Sam – I – am – the – fisher – man,' Alexa giggled and looked at Sam, but he was already busy gulping down his fish and chips.

7

The Secret

Sam's fish was great. 'Sorry your uncle and aunt missed out on the fish, Sam,' Lucy said. 'Now I think it's marshmallow time!'

She got up and went towards the kitchen. 'Mum's got a little stash of them here somewhere,' she said, raising her eyebrows and licking her lips!

'Found them!' she crowed as she came back into the room. She handed each of them a couple of marshmallows on a skewer, and even though they were exhausted they happily sat and watched them melting over the naked flames of the open fire.

'You know what? This reminds me of White Cloud Station!' Alexa said. She was sitting with her arm wrapped around Sam, who wasn't quite sure whether he enjoyed all the attention.

'What's White Cloud Station?' he asked.

'It's where we got our horses from. It's the next best place on earth after this. Well, it's probably equal actually. Every year they round up horses from the high country, and we go there to watch the auction. The last one was the best! We actually got to buy horses of our own. It's the most magical place if you're into horses. You'd really like it, kiddo.'

'One day we're going to be part of the round-up

team,' Suzy said. 'You're not allowed to be in that until you're 16. I can't wait to see Wave again – that's Ripple's mother – that's where he gets his curls from.' She smiled dreamily. 'From his mother's side of the family.'

'Speaking of Wave, you never did finish that story about how she and Ripple got separated from the herd when he was a young. Remember, Suzy? You told us that story at auction time last year?' Lucy rearranged herself on her floor cushion.

'Oh yeah, that's right!' Alexa chimed in. 'You said you'd tell us, and I'm sure Sam would love to hear a good hearty wild horse story, eh – wouldn't you, Sam?' Alexa gave the long-suffering Sam an affectionate tug on one of his ears.

'Sure!' he replied, stuffing a roasted marshmallow in his mouth. 'Suurrre would!'

'Well, for the benefit of Sam I'll start at the beginning.' Suzy smiled, then, getting herself settled by the fire, she began.

'There are wild horses on the hills above White Cloud Station. No one knows exactly how many herds there are because some of them are hidden. We know this because Mitchell has seen them from his helicopter.'

'Wow!' exclaimed Sam. 'Does White Cloud have a chopper?'

'It's not exactly their own. Mitchell lives at Mountain View Village. He flies to the homestead from time to time. When the colts are grown they have to leave the herd, and these outcasts live together in a herd of their own with all the other bachelor colts—'

Sam interrupted her: 'That's not fair! You mean the boys are booted out of the family?'

'Well, yes, I guess it looks a bit that way, Sam,' Suzy giggled. 'But by then they have grown up and it's time to leave home! Besides, some of them form a herd of their own, just the way Koru did. Koru is a beautiful stallion. When Koru is old, another stallion will take over from him.'

'But he wouldn't let another stallion take his herd

away from him, would he?' asked Sam as he reached for another marshmallow.

'I'd say there'd be a bloody good fight!' Alexa stated, clenching her fists like a boxer. Sam laughed and quickly looked back at Suzy, prompting her to continue.

'It's not as bad as it sounds – some colts find mares of their own to form yet another herd! According to the Phillips family, who own White Cloud, there are now several stallions with their own herds. The "Koru Herd", as they call it, is the closest to the station, and Koru is the stallion who's most often seen. Mike Phillips says Koru is a magnificent black. He believes that Koru carries the curly gene.'

Sam was now totally focused and taking in Suzy's every word.

'The horses keep to the far plateaus, as they know they are easy prey in the wide-open pastures. Every herd has an alpha mare; she's the mare who is in charge of each herd. The mare in Ripple's band is wise and old – her name is Destiny, and she's the herd leader.'

'I thought Koru would be the leader?' Sam asked thoughtfully.

'Well, yes, in a way he is. He'll go on ahead or stay behind and fight for his herd if danger approaches, but it's Destiny who actually guides the herd. She's earned this status because she's wise. She knows all there is to know about the best places to eat and where the water holes are. But to get back to the story: Destiny would talk to the foals and prepare them for life in the herd. Koru was the stallion that defended the herd, and even he did as Destiny said. Can you believe that, Sam?'

'Wow, so she would boss him around, eh? My Aunty Kate is like that to Uncle George!' He laughed, sparking off the girls. Then Suzy continued, 'Yes, even some humans are like that, I guess. Dawn and Joe certainly aren't, though – they're very cool!'

'Tell me more about the wild horses!' Sam said, leaning forward eagerly.

'Koru would watch over them and protect them. As the months went by, Ripple and the other foals, his playmates, would venture further away from their mothers and the other members of the herd. Just like you and your friends at boarding school, he had his own group of friends. The foals would play games, just like kids, and gallop and kick up their heels as they breathed in the spring air – it was as if the air contained an energy all of its own. It would even make them silly, and they would spook at weird things like the rustling of leaves in the bushes, or they would imagine they'd seen a tiger, even though there aren't any tigers at White Cloud. The mares would graze nearby, always keeping an eye on their foals; after all, they were really just babies. It's a horse's instinct always to be on the lookout for danger – that's because they're prey animals – and in the wild they would be meat for predators.

'One particular morning, as the wind came up, there was a different smell in the air and the herd became unsettled. Destiny gave out a high-pitched snort, just loud enough to warn the other members of the herd of the danger, but not loud enough for the approaching predator to hear. Destiny knew there was danger – she sensed it!'

'What was scaring her?' Sam asked, his eyes wide.

'Well, you see, Sam, every year there is a round-up. Cowboys and other selected riders go into the hills and bring down some of the horses. The horses rest, they're handled and halter broke, then they are auctioned a day or two later. It was the annual round-up that Destiny could sense – men on horseback were approaching the wild horses at White Cloud Station.' Suzy held out her hand for another marshmallow before continuing.

'Destiny, the lead mare, could see the men on horseback coming towards them. They had one band of horses with them that they had rounded up already, and now they were after her band too. Destiny warned the members of the herd of danger and signalled them to follow her. The tension was building and Koru, the mighty stallion

37

of the herd, was becoming alarmed and agitated. He stood on his hind legs and pawed the air – he was ready for battle!'

'Like Liquorice did today with me?' Sam asked.

'Yes, just like Liqui did today!' Suzy told him, then she went on, 'The herd turned and galloped away. Koru came down from the high rock-face and trotted toward the approaching horsemen. He was protecting his herd as they disappeared around the rock-face and down to the bush and river below. The horsemen were only a few metres away when Koru turned and took flight. He stayed at the rear of his herd to protect them while Destiny led them to safety. Ripple was galloping fast to keep up with his mother, Wave. His legs were already nearly as long as Wave's, and he was well used to the terrain. Suddenly Wave and Ripple separated from the herd, and Wave galloped until she sensed she and her foal were out of danger.

'When she knew it was safe she stopped, and she and her foal stood panting, catching their breaths. She was familiar with this part of the mountain. After all, it was where she had grown up. But she had chosen to live with other horses since the birth of Ripple —'

'I'd like a horse like Ripple one day,' interrupted Sam. 'I'd like to go to White Cloud Station too.'

* * *

'What I'm going to tell you now must never leave this room!' Suzy whispered as she got up and closed the door. 'Agreed?'

All eyes were on her as, in turn, each person nodded solemnly.

'Wave led her foal along a winding track on the side of the misty hill, through a narrow rock arch and into a clearing. And there they were – her mother, her family and several other curly-coated horses. She had returned to them for now, but her heart was with Koru, and she and Ripple belonged with him.

'The curly-coated horses are well hidden high in the ranges, and their coats protect them from the cold. They're highly intelligent, they know what's best for them. They know how to forage for food when the winter sets in, and the safe places to be when the thunder of hooves pounds the valley floor each summer – when the horses with riders come.

'The herd of curlies stay hidden high up in the ranges and no one knows they exist. This incredible herd is kept secret – it's best that way!'

'How do you know this, Suzy?' asked Alexa. 'Horses can't talk and tell stories like this!'

Suzy raised her eyebrows and looked down at Sam. 'What do you think, Sam? Can horses talk?'

'Um, well there are horse whisperers who talk horse language, and they can hear horses talk. So yes, I think they can. Maybe that's their secret – maybe they choose who they want to talk to . . .'

Sam paused and looked into the fire for a moment. 'Besides, sometimes I can hear Ripple talking.'

Suzy nodded in agreement. 'Mm, so you've heard him too? Even when he seems to the other people around him to be silent.'

They smiled at each other, both aware that they shared a special secret, and Sam snuggled deeper into his sleeping bag. He shut his eyes and the corner of his mouth creased to form a tiny smile.

'Sweet horse dreams!' Suzy whispered.

The thunder roared outside, the fire had died down, and the girls and Sam were sprawled on couches and floor rugs in their sleeping bags. It felt good to be safe, and it was good to know their horses were safe in the barn, tucked up in their own blankets and nibbling on fragrant hay. The events of the day had taken their toll, and soon the girls were dozing off as well. By the time the fire died down completely there was no one awake in the room.

8

Good News

The following morning at breakfast Dawn announced that she had spoken earlier with Sam's Aunty Kate and Uncle George. They had invited everyone for lunch, in Sam's honour, and had even been in touch with the media and told them about the rescue. The local newspaper had reacted quickly, keen to publish the story as soon as possible!

It was agreed that the girls would ride over to Sam's place, and Sam would go with Dawn and Joe in the coach. They would all meet around midday.

Later, as Suzy was saddling up Ripple and getting ready to leave, she noticed that Sam was sitting alone, deep in thought. She finished doing up the throat lash on the bridle, and led Ripple over to him as he sat perched on a rock.

'What's wrong, Sam?' she asked.

'Oh, it's Bess,' Sam said, sliding off the rock and walking away with his head lowered. 'I miss her; I'd rather have Bess than any award for bravery.'

'Bess?' Suzy asked, following him.

'She's dead!' he replied, without offering any further information.

Suzy instantly thought of her own mother, who had died four years earlier, and wondered if Sam had also lost his mother. She made a sudden decision.

'Change of plan!' she announced. 'You're riding with me today. Ripple is strong enough to carry both of us, aren't you boy?'

Ripple tossed his head and pawed the ground with a front leg, as if to say, 'Yep, but let's get going.' Suzy took off his saddle and put it in the coach, at the same time letting Joe know about the change of plan. It would be easier if she sat behind Sam on Ripple's bare back – she would let Sam be in charge, he would take the reins. He was a very competent rider, especially for his age, and she already knew she could trust him with her life.

They finally set off, with Liquorice and Hope walking in front of Ripple. After they had gone a little way Alexa turned around in her saddle, almost swinging off the side, and said jokingly, 'Oi, Sam, keep an eye out for the paparazzi – they'll be after you!'

Sam raised his eyebrows and looked around to Suzy. 'Who are they?' he asked nervously.

'They're photographers who chase you when you're famous, and then your photos get splashed across the papers,' Suzy explained.

'Aw, yuk,' Sam said, looking even more concerned.

Sam was controlling Ripple carefully, making sure he kept to a steady pace, and where possible keeping him on the grass verge at the side of the shingle road so he wouldn't get a stone bruise.

'You really miss having a horse on the farm, don't you Sam?'

'Yep, I miss Bess,' Sam replied wistfully, urging Ripple onto a higher grass verge. 'She was an awesome horse!'

Suzy was relieved to know that it wasn't his mother he had been thinking about, but she also knew how much the loss of a much-loved horse could hurt. It was clear that Sam had loved Bess very much.

* * *

The coach was already parked in the driveway of the old farmhouse when the girls and Sam arrived, and Dawn and Joe were being entertained on the front porch under the shade of the veranda.

'I can see the paparazberi,' Sam said anxiously, noticing a strange man with a camera. 'Jeez, what shall we do?'

'You'll be fine, Sam. He's not the paparazzi, he's been invited here – that's different,' Suzy quickly reassured him.

All eyes were on the approaching cavalcade, and as if he was aware of the importance of the visit Ripple rose to the occasion, giving a buck before cantering toward his admiring audience. The journalist snapped a few images as they approached, and Suzy and Sam couldn't help laughing at Ripple's little outburst. After all, horses are allowed to take the lead sometimes, and especially a horse like Ripple with *his* sense of humour. By the time they came to a stop in front of their audience both Suzy and Sam were laughing their heads off. Ripple shook his head up and down, as if joining in, then, spotting a plate of cakes, he leant over and grabbed one in his teeth. Everyone fell about at this, and Ripple seemed quite aware that he was the centre of attention – maybe he just wanted to show people that horses had feelings too!

Sam's anxiety had completely disappeared by this time, and anyway, the 'paparazberi' was much more interested in Ripple than in him!

* * *

Kate and George couldn't help but notice the big change in Sam's demeanour – it was as if Ripple had turned on a light inside the boy and brought back 'their Sam', the bubbly, cheerful boy they used to know.

Sam came to live with Kate and George when he

was seven. His father, George's brother, sailed off to see the world following his wife's death. George found it difficult to understand how his brother could abandon his child so callously. It broke his heart to see young Sam looking out from Castle Point in anticipation of seeing his father's yacht return. George decided to get Sam a horse and his neighbours offered their farm horse, Bess. They noticed within a short while how the old mare lifted his spirits – but then tragically Bess had died. Since then something had been missing in Sam's life, and he had become sad and withdrawn. Kate and George had decided it would be better for him to go to boarding school and mix with other children – at least that way he would have the chance to make more friends than he could at the isolated farm. Besides, they knew he would be able to see horses at the West Grove riding school.

What they hadn't realised was that Sam needed to have a horse of his own, one he could care for, love and train the way he had with Bess. Sam had taught Bess to jump and do tricks, and more importantly, she was the one he turned to when life was mean. Bess would always listen and help him understand the world.

Suzy could tell that horses were in Sam's blood, and that like her, the energy horses gave out flowed through his veins. The other thing she knew about Sam was that he was a *natural* in the presence of horses; this was clearly obvious to Ripple, and Suzy had picked up on it too. She wondered if Mike had been like this at a similar age, and the thought helped her make a decision.

She would email Mike, using Dawn's laptop, and arrange for Sam to visit White Cloud Station while he was still on holiday. With her part-time jobs at her father's surgery, and at the stables owned by Alexa's parents, she had earned enough money to buy a horse. She would organise it so that Sam again had his own horse – a White Cloud horse! She knew Mike was due back at the station in two weeks, and that he would also recognise the instinctive bond Sam had with horses. After all, Mike had given her Ripple, hadn't he?

'Sam,' she said quietly, 'come over here. They have facilities for horses at your boarding school, don't they?'

Sam nodded, not really seeing the point of her question.

'You saved our lives, Ripple and I, and we want to thank you from the bottom of our hearts.

'And now we've got some good news for you . . .'

9

One Door Closes

Suzy felt sad as she closed the door to Horse Heaven. All too soon their beach holiday had come to an end, and it was time to focus on the future. She needed to learn her dressage test, which she had to ride from memory, and do more pole work with Ripple, and she felt a little overwhelmed at how much she needed to do in preparation for the upcoming Highfield horse trials. This was no ordinary event; if she did well she would qualify to represent her area at the National Pony Club Championships. If they made the team she and Ripple would be competing against the best in the country at her level.

This was her dream, and if it came true it would put her in line for selection the following year, when Ripple would be in a higher grade. It could mean she would soon be representing her country at the top level. She dreamed of taking Ripple to the Badminton horse trials and even the Olympics – and why not, she thought. After all, she already knew dreams could come true!

Suzy and Ripple made a good team as they were both focused and determined when it came to eventing. Suzy was also thrilled to have found an instructor who was so experienced in eventing and dressage. Netty had heaps of experience, and Suzy liked the way she was so kind to the horses. In many ways she reminded Suzy of Mike, who had given Ripple his early training, and this made her comfortable. And even better, Netty lived at Jasmine Farm, where Suzy kept Ripple.

Netty had high hopes for Suzy and Ripple, and she was pleased with the progress they had made over the past few months. Ripple was working well under saddle and maintained a nice contact on the bit. He also had an elegance all of his own, and Netty was not surprised that he had impressed the judges at the events they had competed in so far. 'He's got presence, this horse,' she would say to Suzy. 'He's going to turn some heads!'

Ripple seemed to grow a hand higher when he entered through the gates of the arena, as if to say, 'Look at me – here I come!' Throughout his tests he would maintain a soft outline and happily work on the bit. He had cadence, good paces and an even rhythm. All of the groundwork Suzy had done, with Mike's help, transferred through to his dressage – he was soft and supple. And with the interval training she had done on the beach she knew he had the stamina for the enduring cross-country phase. His jumping style was tidy and he tucked up neatly over the larger fences – he was bold, with a good length of stride, and he covered the ground well, so time faults were not too much of a worry either. Suzy felt quite confident about the showjumping. This final part of the competition often tripped up tired horses, but she was focused on Ripple's fitness and was not fazed by this – she felt positive and ready! She so wanted Ripple to do well; she so wanted Mike to be proud of them, and she sooo wanted to compete at national level.

She was looking forward to visiting White Cloud again too, and hoped she would be able to take Sam and that Mike would agree to choose a horse for him. She had emailed Mike, but hadn't heard back yet.

With her pack over her shoulder she walked down the path, the shells crunching under her sneakers, closed the gate behind her, and went toward the coach. She laughed as she got closer and looked up to see three sets of eyes looking out at her through the windows of the horse compartment. It was as if they were saying, 'C'mon, Suzy, we're all waiting for you – let's get this show on the road!'

As she climbed up the steps into the coach, she turned and took one last look back over to the cave and above it to Castle Point. Her eyes scanned the cliff-face, then followed the beach back to HH where poor old Bones was standing all alone, looking out to the huge ocean. The last of her sadness quickly

passed, and she turned back toward Lucy and Alexa, waiting for her in the living area. 'D'you think old Bones will weather a winter okay without us?'

'I dunno,' Lucy laughed, 'he's a bit light in condition! But he's well boned and strong – and he's a good doer.'

'Anyway, the coach can only take three horses – SORRY BONES!' Alexa yelled out the open window as she waved farewell to Bones. 'We declare you the official caretaker of HH. See you next summer!'

Still laughing, the girls took their seats in the living area, and Joe turned the ignition key. The green light came on and the motor turned over and purred. When he reached the gateway Joe stopped momentarily out of habit, checking left and right that Dusty Road was clear. Suzy wasn't sure why he hesitated so long – no one else ever used the road.

As they rumbled down Dusty Road, Dawn broke the silence by leaning over from her seat in the cab and holding out an A4 sheet of paper. Pretending it was of no consequence, she handed the paper to Suzy. 'Oh, this came for you this morning, Suzy. I printed it out for you. Thought it would be good reading on the trip!' She smiled.

Suzy took the piece of paper. It was an email:

Hi Suzy

Hey, no problem – Sam can choose himself a horse. I'll be home next week and I'll bring in a little palomino I backed a few months ago. She's a really awesome little mare, she was working nicely. She's soft in the mouth so she'll need a sympathetic type of rider – someone with kind hands. She's not too big either, and she's good-natured. She'd be my pick at this stage, unless Sam wants to wait until after the auction? Doubt that. I'll work her and she'll be ready for Sam to ride when he gets to White Cloud. There's also a pretty liver chestnut gelding, but somehow I don't think it would be Sam's pick. I'll give him some lessons while he's there – no worries!

Anyhow, just cruise on up when you guys are ready! I phoned Grandma and she's

invited you to stay – as you know, there're
plenty of spare rooms in the big house.

It'll be great seeing you again.

Gotta fly, Mike.

Nearly forgot, be sure to bring Ripple – you
can get his fitness levels up over the hills and
there're plenty of cross-country jumps.

Wow! Suzy thought. Mike had really given this some thought.
He was so kind, and she was impressed by how willing he
was to help Sam find the right horse. He hadn't even met Sam
yet! She leant back and quietly opened the door to the horse
compartment, where the horses were standing diagonally, each
looking out of their own little window.

'Hey Ripple,' she whispered, 'more summer adventures
to come!'

PART 2

Return to White Cloud Station

10

Mist

It wasn't until she looked down and saw the White Cloud homestead in the far distance that Suzy realised how far into the hills she and Ripple had climbed. Looking at her watch she was amazed that half the morning had passed without her noticing – it was already 10.30. She took her drink bottle out of her saddlebag, and in between sips she looked out over the expanse of land spread before her. She could just make out the White Cloud homestead, the river, and the road leading to the station. It felt good to be back at White Cloud Station, especially at this time of the year – it felt familiar and the auction was just around the corner. Suzy had a few days' riding time before then, and today she'd decided to set off early so she could be back at the homestead around midday. Mike would be back from Mountain View Village by then. He was picking up his grandfather who had spent the night in the medical centre for his annual check-up and Suzy was looking forward to finally meeting Grandad Phillips.

She dismounted, loosened Ripple's girth and took off the saddlebag, then she slipped off his bridle as he was finding it difficult to eat with the bit in his mouth. Putting the bridle on the rock beside her, she sat down and leant against the rock, enjoying the sight of the world spread out before her. She tilted her head, admiring her horse's beauty, and asked him, 'Where are we, Ripple?'

Ripple kept munching the mountain grass, not at all concerned about where they were.

Suzy reached into her pocket for the map Mike had sketched for her. She wasn't sure if they had gone beyond the tracks he had drawn. He had warned her that it was easy to get lost in the vastness of the ranges, and also that the weather patterns up there could be changeable and the nights much colder than down below.

Ripple happily grazed while Suzy felt around in her pocket for the map. She emptied both her pockets and laid the contents on the grass in front of her crossed legs. There was her scrunched neck scarf, a few barley sugars, and that was it. Puzzled, she reached over and rummaged around in her saddle-bag, then tipped out the contents. There on the ground lay a pack of sandwiches, another drink bottle, some baling twine, a muesli slice, her sweater and her inhaler – but no map!

'Well, Ripple, we'll have to follow our tracks back down!' she said, trying to reassure herself that they would be okay. But it didn't work! She was starting to feel quite panicky about the situation, and she could tell her breathing was about to give her grief. Feeling an asthma attack coming on, she quickly took two puffs of her inhaler and leant back against the rock. When I feel more settled, she thought, we'll make our way back down. I mean, how hard can that be?

She looked down at the homestead and decided, All I have to do is head in that direction!

After a few minutes she called Ripple, tightened the girth and put his bridle back on, then they embarked on their trek back to the homestead. But Ripple hesitated as Suzy tried to steer him to the left. Then he stopped altogether, and when Suzy urged him on he refused and pawed at the ground as if he was having a tantrum.

'Ripple, please!' Suzy said desperately. 'We have to

stick to this track. Come on, this isn't like you.' She urged him on by squeezing his sides, and he reluctantly walked forward. 'Good boy, that's better!' she muttered.

Suzy reached back to the side of her saddle and pulled out her sweatshirt. Throwing the reins on Ripple's wither, she stretched her arms in the air and put the sweatshirt on. She knew Netty wouldn't approve of her doing that, but stuff like that didn't worry Ripple. Besides, waves of mist were starting to appear and she was feeling a lot cooler than before.

As they continued along the track they came to an unusual rock formation. It was hard to see clearly through the mist, but it looked like an archway. Oh-oh, Suzy thought, I definitely don't remember seeing this on the way up!

The mist was now sweeping lower around them and an eerie feeling came over Suzy as they stopped before the arch. 'Gawd, Ripple, we're LOST!'

Ripple was now pawing the ground so intensely that he was bouncing Suzy up and down. 'What's wrong, boy? I've never seen you like this.'

She felt unnerved and gathered in his reins in a way she normally wouldn't. Ripple started prancing about on the spot making unusual soft nickering noises then, pulling the reins out of her hands, he spun around. He trotted toward the arch, his body tense and his head high, then he swept them both under and through it. Suzy couldn't see much but she could sense something strange, something eerie; there was a presence that gave her goose bumps.

Ripple stopped suddenly. 'C'mon, Ripple, let's get out of here, I'm not liking this – there's something creepy about this place!'

She gathered up the reins and squeezed Ripple's sides, but he didn't move. He planted his feet and his whole body quivered as he let out a high-pitched call!

'Ripple, please, you're scaring me!' Suzy sobbed, feeling increasingly desperate.

Suddenly, floating straight toward them in the mist, was a horse ghost! Suzy had never felt so vulnerable and alone. Terrified, she froze as the apparition came closer. Ripple quivered, his neck arched and his ears pointed in the direction of the ghost horse.

What's going on? I didn't think ghosts had shadows! Suzy was becoming more and more confused. She felt peculiar, as if she was in a waking dream, yet she now felt no fear as the ghost horse's eyes, ears and then neck appeared out of the heavy mist. The apparition stretched its nose and lightly touched Ripple's, and with a high-pitched nicker it turned into a living horse! There in front of Suzy's eyes was the most beautiful horse she had ever seen. It greeted Ripple with pricked ears and flared nostrils. Suzy sat motionless, and speechless, observing as the two horses communicated silently. Suzy wondered what they were saying to each other in their own special equine language.

The mist drifted apart for a moment and Suzy saw that the horse had a foal at her side. For the first time, she could also see the bay horse clearly. 'Wave?' She said uncertainly, finally making the connection. 'Wave, is that you?'

Suzy felt strange, as if she was an intruder. This place belongs to Ripple's family, she thought, and Ripple is happy to be back. Feeling overwhelmed and confused she leant forward, swung her leg over Ripple's back and started to dismount. Ripple didn't even seem to notice. He was totally focused on Wave. 'This is where you want to be, isn't it?' Ripple pawed the ground. 'I knew it!' she murmured.

As Suzy slid to the ground Wave took her foal back a few steps and circled him, as if to put a barrier between him and the predator.

'I won't hurt your baby, Wave!' Suzy reassured her, then she reached up and pulled Ripple's saddle off his back. She took off his bridle and stepped back, tears in her eyes.

'Off you go, Ripple,' she said sadly. 'This is where you belong!'

Ripple trotted over to Wave, who turned and began to walk away into the mist. Ripple stopped suddenly, turned back as if to say a final farewell, lifted his head high and neighed. Then he too disappeared into the mist.

Suzy looked down at her saddle then slowly collapsed in a heap beside it, sobbing. As she wiped her runny nose and eyes on her sleeve, she thought desperately, Ripple doesn't love me! He'd rather be up here than with me!

Oh gawd, how am I ever going to explain this to Mike? That's if I ever get back to the homestead – I'm lost in the mist!

As she sobbed her heart out she couldn't help thinking what a disaster this had turned out to be. She was supposed to be fulfilling her dream of a lifetime, with the horse she loved most in the world and with people who had been so kind to her, and now she had no horse to share her dreams with! They're going to be so disappointed, she thought. The tears were still streaming down her face, and as quickly as she wiped them away more came.

She reached out and pulled her jacket from the back of the saddle, and put it on. Mike was right about it getting cold. Then she curled up and covered her body with Ripple's saddle blanket. The smell of him on the cloth made her cry even harder. She huddled on the ground, shivering with cold and grief, and resting her head on the saddle. She felt as if she was going to die. Her heart was broken, and she felt totally exhausted. Despite the cold she started to doze off, worn out by her emotions.

Suddenly she felt something crawling over her chin. She dared not move for fear it was a massive spider or something equally scary. She felt it crawl over her cheek then up to her eyebrow, and still she dared not move. Finally, petrified, she opened one of her eyes. Two big eyes looked back at her. She sat bolt upright, hardly able to believe her eyes!

'Ripple!'

Ripple nudged her, as if to say 'Get up!' She stood up and stroked his nose.

'You came back of your own accord! Oh Ripple, I love you so much. Thank you for coming back!'

By now the mist had lifted, and Suzy decided she should get moving while she could see. She saddled Ripple up quickly and mounted him. They wove their way back along the track and under the archway, Ripple striding along confidently. Suzy was relieved that he seemed to know the way, as she had totally lost her bearings!

'I'll leave it to you, boy – you know the way home, don't you? You tried to tell me earlier! I should have taken more notice.'

Ripple veered off the track and climbed down a steep slope, then headed along another narrow track on the edge of a hill. The soothing motion of his walk and the heat of the day made Suzy feel pleasantly sleepy. The track took them further down into the hills and Suzy could see what looked like a hut in the distance. She couldn't quite understand what a hut would be doing in the middle of nowhere, but then she didn't really know where nowhere was since she was lost! As they got closer she could see it looked like a musterer's hut, and although it lacked the artist's touch it reminded her of Horse Heaven. There was a hitching rail outside beside another smaller shelter, as well as some stockyards.

Ripple seemed to know where he was heading, and Suzy let him have his head. He stopped at the hitching rail, and Suzy wrapped her lead rope over the rail and headed towards the hut.

The door creaked as she slowly opened it, and as she peeked inside she could see several sets of rough-looking wooden bunks, a table made of what looked like a slab of tree trunk, and in the far corner what appeared to be a kind of kitchen area, with a bench and some shelves. There was another rough wooden table and some stools, which looked as if they had been made by cavemen. Suzy stepped inside and walked over to the bench. There was a collection of containers and tins on the shelves, and Suzy ran her fingers along them as she read the labels.

The hut had a welcoming feel to it and was obviously still used by someone, she thought. On a rough-sawn timber shelf above the stone fireplace there were even some books, an old lantern and some candles. Suzy was slightly puzzled that an old hut in the middle of nowhere should be so well set up; there was even bedding on the old bunks. She wondered if it was waiting for visitors. She sat down on one of the beds and giggled – this must have been what Goldilocks felt like when she stumbled into the three bears' house! Suzy thought she better leave before they returned! Her mood was lifting and she walked back outside.

Suzy loved the way Ripple nickered out to her – she had never quite figured out how he knew she was coming, but he always called before she was in sight. 'Ripple,' she said, giving him a rub. 'You're waiting patiently, good boy!'

'Right, Ripple,' she said, 'let's get going. We need to be back at the station. They'll be back by now! Mike will be wondering where we are. Oh and Grandad Phillips will be waiting to meet us too!'

* * *

Ripple took them back down to the plateau without any drama, and Suzy felt relieved to be back in a part of the countryside she recognised. She let out a sigh, and in response Ripple gave a small buck, as if to say, 'Come on – let's go!'

He must have been reading Suzy's mind, as she had spotted some interesting-looking logs ahead, just right for some jumping practice on the way down!

11

Communication

By the time Suzy and Ripple arrived back at White Cloud it was late-afternoon. They found Mike walking toward the round yard.

'Hi Suzy, I hope you had an enjoyable ride. You've been away a long time – hope you didn't get lost!' he laughed.

Suzy thought of her mother's saying, 'Many a true word spoken in jest', and replied simply, 'Yes, it was great, thanks Mike!'

'Whew!' he sighed. 'I was beginning to worry about the two of you, especially when I noticed the mist coming in. Anyhow, you're both safe. I'm just about to give Sam a lesson – do you want to join us?'

'Sounds great!' Suzy replied. 'I'll just sort Ripple out and be over soon.'

After unsaddling Ripple she tied the lead rope in a quick-release knot around the rail and reached for the body brush from her grooming kit. Looking over Ripple's back as she brushed him, she could see Mike was now with Sam and a palomino in the round yard.

'A bit of a nip in the air today, lass; we get this cool nip, comes in with that mist up there. But don't you be worried, it'll be gone in a day or three!'

Suzy turned quickly to see who had spoken. The old man smiled as he walked past, leaning heavily on his walking stick. Before Suzy had time to respond he was powering off towards the round yard.

'Excuse me,' Suzy called, running after him, 'I'm Suzy; you must be . . . ?'

'I know who you are, lass! I'll be talking to you later. Got something important to attend to!' The old man kept walking toward the round yard.

This wasn't the introduction Suzy had anticipated having with Grandad Phillips. She tried to figure out why he had been so abrupt as she walked back to Ripple, who was now pulling at the knot on the rail. 'You horses are much easier to deal with than humans sometimes!' Ripple nudged her, as if to agree, or maybe to show her he had untied his knot!

'What good is a quick-release knot when a horse knows how to use it to his advantage!' she laughed.

* * *

Suzy returned Ripple to his paddock, taking advantage of the extra time to compose herself before she joined the others at the round yard. Mike and the old man were leaning on the rail looking in. Suzy's face lit up, mirroring the expression on Sam's face as he rode a young hack around the yard. He glanced at her momentarily, then just as quickly focused back on the small horse he was riding. Suzy also focused on the palomino, realising it was the horse she had shared her troubles with at the auction the previous year, when she had been worrying about whether her father would let her bid for Ripple.

'Okay, that's great, Sam,' Mike called. 'Now quietly urge her on into a trot, a gentle nudge on her sides, and keep only a light contact on the reins.' Sam did this perfectly and the mare responded, trotting freely around the yard. 'Again, Sam, and into a canter!'

With one eye on Sam and one on Suzy, Mike introduced her to the old man: 'Grandad, this is Suzy.'

'Yes, I know; pleased to meet you,' the old man smiled and held out a weathered hand.

Suzy looked the old gentleman in the eyes and smiled back at him. 'Pleased to meet you officially, Grandad. Oh, sorry – should I call you Grandad?' she asked, feeling slightly embarrassed.

'Of course you can call me Grandad, lass,' the old man chuckled. 'I've been called plenty of other names, but that's how I'm known round here – Grandad Phillips.'

'Well then, pleased to meet you, Grandad!'

Grandad smiled, but his attention had already returned to Sam, who was now doing the cooling down exercises Mike had taught him.

'Very good, lad,' he told the boy, 'very good riding!' He turned back to Suzy. 'Mike tells me you'll be buying the horse for this young man, lass?'

'Yes, that's right, Grandad, if that's the one he wants. Is this your pick, Sam?'

'Sure is!'

Suzy looked at Grandad and nodded. 'Will you let me know how much you want for him, and I'll do an electronic payment to your bank account.'

'Oh phh, all that computer stuff! Emails and yPods! I don't know . . . what's the world coming to? All these new ways of communicating – people have forgotten how to *talk* to each other . . .'

'It's iPods, Grandad,' Suzy corrected him, giggling as she realised his gruff way of talking was just part of his nature.

'Mmm,' the old man grunted, 'iPods, yPods, all the same to me! Give me nature any day, lass. Nature, horses and good Scotch whisky, that's what God intended us to have.'

He gave her a little smile, and she noticed a slight sparkle in his eyes as he gathered up his walking stick and headed back toward the homestead. It seemed to Suzy that seeing the horses had refreshed him, and he no longer looked his 90 years.

'Grandma Phillips will be expecting you all for dinner at six. Doesn't do to keep her waiting!' he called back, laughing.

'Does she get stroppy, like Aunt Kate does when Uncle George is late in for his dinner?' called Sam, who had a bird's-eye view of the old man from the top of the palomino.

'Grr, I'll stroppy you! You worry about that horse under you, and not about what's going on around you. When you're up on the back of a horse that's where your focus should be, and don't you forget it!' The old man winked as he walked away.

* * *

'Don't worry, guys,' Mike said reassuringly, 'his bark's worse than his bite!'

'Eek,' shrugged Suzy, 'I sure hope so. I felt a bit awkward. I thought he didn't like me!'

'Yeah, he likes you; he just has a funny way of showing his emotions. Communication isn't his strong point with people, but he's brilliant at it with horses! Gotta remember he's lived up here pretty isolated except for the shepherds and horsemen who come and go – he's a bit of a loner – says he can't be bothered with a lot of folk, that horses have more brains most of the time . . . He likes you all right, Suzy – after all, it was *he* who told the guy in the black hat to bid for Ripple at the auction.'

Suzy thought back to the day of the auction when she had seen Ripple bought by a mysterious stranger in a dark hat. It was only later, when Ripple turned up at Jasmine Farm, that she learnt the stranger had been Mike – bidding for Ripple as a gift for her after seeing the special bond she and the horse shared.

Feeling moved as she remembered his generosity, she was unable to answer Mike. She kept her mouth tightly closed, her lips quivering, knowing that if she dared move them she would blurt out the world's loudest blubbering noise – which was not what she wanted to do in front of Mike and Sam!

She composed herself and managed her best-ever appreciative smile. 'I'll always be grateful to Grandad Phillips,' she said, desperately hoping the two of them weren't thinking, Oh, that's emotional girls for you!

Sam dismounted from the palomino.

'They did really well today,' Mike remarked to Suzy, taking off his hat and wiping his brow. 'I'm positive they'll be good together. Seems the two of them really connect.'

'Thanks, Mike; this means so much to me,' Suzy replied. 'I remember this mare from the auction; was she passed in?'

'Well, to be honest . . .' Mike laughed sheepishly. 'I actually pulled her out as I thought I'd keep her myself.'

After he had rubbed down the palomino and put her in the paddock beside Ripple's, Sam returned to where Mike and Suzy were picking up manure from in and around the yard.

'C'mon, let's go get some grub – I'm so hungry I could eat an H O R . . .' he shrieked joyfully.

'Don't you dare say "horse", you ratbag,' laughed Suzy, jokingly swinging the full manure shovel at him. Sam took off away from her, not sure how good her aim was.

'Anyhow, how come we're cleaning up after *your* new horse, Sam?' Mike asked him. 'You should be shovelling your own horse shit!'

'Mrs Stevenson at the riding school would say *manuuuure*, not shit!' Sam giggled.

'Well, they've certainly pointed you in the right direction with your equitation skills, Sam. Their approach might be slightly different to how you would do things now that you're a cowboy, but it's all the same really. You have quite a combination of skills and ways with horses for a kid. I'm impressed.'

Serious now, Sam replied, 'Bess taught me best. Bess *was* the best!'

'One day you'll love another horse as much as you loved Bess,' Mike reassured him. 'I remember when I was little I lost my best dog. I never thought I'd love another dog the way I loved Handy, but I do.

'C'mon,' he added, 'we've got to get showered before dinner. We'd better get cracking.'

'What do us cowboys wear to posh dinners?' Sam asked, cheerful again.

As they turned to walk toward the homestead the palomino whinnied.

Sam stopped and looked back. 'You know what, Mike?' he asked thoughtfully.

'What?' Mike smiled.

'I reckon Bess is now *second* best!'

12

Dining in Style

All eyes turned to Suzy as she walked into the dining room.

'Cor, Suzy, I didn't know you wore dresses!' Sam exclaimed. 'You look quite pretty!'

'Thanks, Sam,' Suzy replied, blushing slightly. 'You've scrubbed up pretty well too,' she added, leaning over and pinching his cheek as she sat down beside him.

The table was set elegantly with beautiful china, and Suzy noticed that the White Cloud emblem was engraved on the handles of the silver cutlery. A woman she hadn't seen before came in and placed some serving spoons on the table in front of them.

'Is she a servant?' Sam asked as the woman went out.

'Cynthia and her husband Ron have lived at White Cloud Station for twenty years, Sam – even before Mike was born,' Grandad explained. 'Cynthia works here in the house, and Ron helps out on the farm with the stockmen and shepherds.

'We're all servants to White Cloud in a sense. Everybody is as important as the next person – that's the way it is here. Everyone is necessary and has a job to do, just as the horses and working dogs do. The horses and dogs can go places motorbikes can't – without the horses we'd not be able to get up to some of the ranges. Some of those hills are steep and that's part of the reason we need to ride horses to round up the wild ones. Sometimes wild horses are rounded up by helicopters but we don't do that here. We believe our method is less stressful and we have more control over the herds. Speaking of the round-up it's just around the corner and we need really strong, healthy horses.'

'Oh, boy, I'd love to join in the ride, wouldn't you Suzy?'

'Are you kidding? It'd be awesome! Only one problem, Sammy boy, you and I aren't old enough! I guess my arms aren't quite long enough to reach the stars yet!'

They fell silent as the food was brought in and the smell of country cooking wafted around the room.

'All home grown, I'll have you know,' Grandad Phillips said as he started to carve the roast meat. 'I may not do as much riding as I used to but I sure know how to grow food for this table!'

'Yum, roast beef and crunchy roast potatoes – my favourites! And all grown here at White Cloud, Grandad?' Sam nodded and licked his lips.

While Grandad was carving, Mike poured champagne into fluted glasses.

'Now,' Grandma said, looking round the table, 'I want to hear all about how the horses went today, starting with Ripple.'

'First, my dear,' Grandad interrupted, 'a toast!' He stood up and lifted his wine glass. 'To friends old and new. To the horses we are privileged to have in our lives. And to my beautiful wife.'

'Thank you, my dear,' Grandma smiled and sipped her champagne.

Sam took a sip from his own fizzy drink and added, 'And to champagne bubbles up my nose.'

The others all laughed as his comical expression.

'Well, how was your horse today, young man?' Grandma asked. 'Have you thought of a name for her yet?

'Champagne Bubbles?' Sam suggested with a giggle.

'Well,' Grandma replied, laughing, 'now – that's a very colourful name!'

* * *

When it was Suzy's turn she was careful to avoid any mention of getting lost. She described how she had taken Ripple up toward the eastern plateau in anticipation of finding some wild horses, and was slightly relieved when Mike interrupted her.

'You won't find any up there at this time of the year – they'll be hiding out. The older mares get to know when the round-up is nearing. With just a few days to go they'll be well hidden away!'

'Anyway,' Suzy continued, 'we had a gallop up on the ridge on the way home, and I found some neat logs to jump in the back paddock. Ripple just takes them in his stride. I'm really looking forward to the Highfield Horse Trials!' She smiled at Grandad, who gave a small nod of approval.

'Yes, I saw you jumping Ripple,' he said, taking a sip of wine. 'Very nicely done, I might add.'

Suzy's smile widened.

'Now you make sure you keep a check on that horse of yours,' Grandad went on. 'Make sure he's listening to you; while it's good if he's keen, Suzy, you must be the one in control. He's confident and looking for the next fence, and that's how it should be. A jumping horse needs to be enjoying his job! But he'll be depending on you for reassurance and guidance . . .' He put down his glass and held up his hands as if he was riding. 'Now this is a bounce, Ripple, you must say, I want you to shorten up your stride and . . .'

'I didn't know you did jumping too, Grandad?' Suzy was impressed.

Grandad winked at her and replied, 'I know a "little" bit.'

'Grandad's teasing you, Suzy, he used to jump a lot!' Mike laughed. There wasn't much the old man didn't know about horse riding and equines.

'Just watch out for some of these new fandangled ideas about horsemanship and riding. Now, horses are horses! But sometimes things turn full circle, lass. Most of these new ways of working with horses – they're really old.'

'As old as you, Grandad?' Sam asked innocently.

'Yes, boy,' the old man chuckled, 'as old as me! We've been working horses this way at White Cloud since I was a kid. Now young Mike here is learning the same ways of working with horses, except some of these "clinicians" give it a fancy new name. I've seen a lot of different ways of working with horses over my many years, and I'll tell you what, I know some old fellas who have been teaching horses this way for years – nah, it's not new. They've branded it and are using it to make money. It can't be bought . . .'

Mike laughed. 'Oh no, now you've got him started!'

'Horse-handling skills and riding come more naturally to some than to others – but we can all learn how to improve. Like Grandma here, she's a natural on the piano, she doesn't even need sheet music – she just sits down and the music vibrates through your body, and enters your very soul. That's what happens to a good horseman, like Mike here. He's a natural around horses, they're in his blood.' Grandad looked across at Suzy. 'That's the way it will be with you and Ripple, lass, at this event – you must become as one with that horse of yours.'

'I'll try, Grandad. I really want to qualify for the championships, and I want to win!'

'Well, it's not all about winning the trophy, Suzy; it's about how you win. And more importantly, it's about winning your horse's heart. Prizes come and go, but winning your horse, well, that's the biggest prize of all. A horse that wants to work with you is a great gift.'

'So, don't you think I should be competing with Ripple yet, Grandad?' Suzy asked, slightly confused.

'Not at all, lass, but have the right intentions. By all means compete, just be sure your horse is happy too – ensure he's feeling the same way – it needs to be fun for both of you.'

'Oh, I get it. Yes, of course – Ripple's well-being comes first. Always!'

'There's plenty of time. You must quietly work your way up the grades – you know, those top Olympic horses don't get there by rushing. It takes a long time to build up that relationship – no rush, lass; no rush.'

'Okay, yeah, thanks Grandad.'

'Now, what say we all sit outside on the veranda and watch the sun go down – and let our meals go down too.' Grandad smiled and got up slowly. 'I'm ready for a cigar!'

They followed the old man outside and settled down on the veranda. The view was breathtaking. Suzy looked up to the hills where the herds of wild horses would be grazing. She wondered what they would be doing, how many there would be and where the *other* curly horses would be hiding out? As she glanced down over the yards, the barn and the stable block, she could see Ripple and Mike's horse Flair grazing below in the house paddock. She could see Bubbles in the paddock beside them, and a flutter of happiness ran through her body. She looked along the veranda beside her, and the happiness grew – she had friends old and new, and great horses in her life.

She missed Alexa and Lucy, and she was making mental notes of all the things she wanted to share with them in her email later in the evening – she had promised to let them know what was happening at the station.

'I can see a big white cloud in the shape of a horse – look, look up there!' Sam said, jumping up and pointing to a cloud above the hill. 'Now I know why this is called White Cloud Station. Man, this is awesome!'

13

A Special Gift

The sun put on an impressive display, turning the sky different tones of pink as it fell behind the hills, ending the day on a perfect note. As darkness fell Grandma Phillips got up, bidding them all good night, and asked Mike to escort her to her room.

When he returned to the veranda a little later he told Suzy, 'Grandma would like you to go and say goodnight.' He gave her directions to his grandmother's room, and Suzy made her way up the stairs. On the landing a beautiful painting of a young woman caught her eye. She stopped and stared in awe, noticing the detail of the tapered riding jacket the woman was wearing. She also noticed how the woman's eyes matched the colour of the stunning turquoise necklace that hung around her neck and rested softly on her hunting stock. As she leant forward for a closer look she saw that the necklace was engraved with the letters 'WC'.

'That was a long time ago, my darling,' a voice behind her said quietly. 'Yes, a long time ago. I was only 17 when my parents had that painted – not much older than you, Suzy.'

Suzy jumped. 'You're wearing a riding habit, Grandma.'

'Yes,' replied the old lady. 'I sometimes chose to

ride side-saddle. I used to go to a lot of shows, and like you I loved my jumping. I had some nice hunters and used them for stock work as well.

'Now come with me, girl; I'm tired and I need to rest.'

Suzy followed her down the long hallway, passing a number of rooms before they reached Grandma's door. Grandma reached out and turned the shiny brass handle, opening the large wooden door to her bedroom. Suzy noticed the 'WC' again, this time carved on the door.

'Come in and sit down over here, Suzy,' Grandma said, leading the way to a small, ornately carved table with matching chairs.

'Do you ever miss riding, Grandma?' Suzy asked as she sat down.

'Indeed I do, Suzy,' the old lady replied, pouring herself a small glass of sherry from a crystal decanter. 'Oh yes, those were the days; long rides up into the hills – Koru Falls, the eastern plateau, the wild horses – I do miss going up there.'

'I haven't heard about Koru Falls, Grandma,' Suzy said enquiringly as she sat down opposite her. She felt unusually elegant in her dress and heels, and she sat up straight, neatly crossing her ankles.

'Yes dear, it's near Musterer's Hut,' Grandma replied closing her eyes.

'Koru Falls,' Grandma said dreamily, and as though travelling back in time she continued, 'That was certainly one very special day.'

'How so?'

'Grandad and I had ridden up to the falls, and while the horses rested and picked at the grass we swam in the cool, clear water. So refreshing – we ducked and dived like a couple of teenagers.'

Suzy laughed. 'That's so cute, Grandma!'

Grandma laughed with her, then she continued, 'It's beautiful, Suzy; you can swim behind the waterfall and there's a hidden cave – one day you'll see it.' She paused. 'I guess you've had enough of caves for now, though; my goodness, that must have been an experience for you. But you're a sensible girl . . .' She sipped her sherry. 'Later we sat at the water's edge and watched the cascade of water falling over the precipice above – like liquid silk falling into the pool below.' She paused and raised her hands, as if she had seen something. 'And suddenly there she was, with her neck arched like a stallion, walking on her toes as if not touching the earth below, circling her newborn foal and warning us not to come near her. She gave a little nicker and Grandad grabbed my arm to stop me moving toward her. We both just stood there, captivated by their beauty.'

'Oh Grandma, how exciting!'

'There was an eclipse that night, so we named her Eclipse. What a sight to behold, a mare protecting her newborn, warning both our horses and us not to come any closer.'

Suzy knew exactly what she meant. She too had felt the might of a protective mare, and she got a flash of Wave with her young colt in the mist.

'It's not often the wild ones come down to the hut area, but there she was, and there he was on his wobbly legs beside her.'

'Who, Grandma?

'Koru, Ripple's sire. We named the falls after him. He was the most beautiful colt I've ever seen, with his curly little tail and mane. He didn't keep his curls, not like Ripple's at least.'

'That's such a beautiful story. You must have so many incredible stories. Will you tell me more some time?' Suzy studied her, in her mind comparing her to the young woman in the painting. She had the sudden thought that old people are just young people in old people's bodies. She felt she had a new girlfriend.

'Yes of course, anytime, darling. I was just like you, you know. Horses were, and still are, I might add, in my blood and they will always be in my life. Now that

I can't ride I get pleasure from watching Mike, and now of course I have you and little Sam to watch as well. There's such freedom on the back of a horse. I would not have traded White Cloud for the world!'

She put her empty glass on the table and stood up, then she recited:

'Take the life of cities!
Here's the life for me.
'Twere a thousand pities not to gallop free.
So we'll ride together, Comrade, you and I
careless of the weather, letting care go by.'

'Who wrote that, Grandma? It's beautiful!' Suzy sighed.

'I don't know, darling. I've read so many books in my lifetime,' she laughed, 'I can't remember half of them. I guess they're tucked away in here.' She pointed to her head.

'I've a library full of horse books. If ever you want a book, you know you can visit the library and help yourself.'

'Thanks, Grandma. I'd love to. I love reading!' Suzy got up, thinking the old lady must be getting tired. 'Maybe I could go and have a look now.'

'Just a minute, Suzy! I need to lie down, but there's something I want to show you. Do you mind if I get changed for bed?'

'Of course not,' Suzy said, sitting down again.

Grandma got up and went behind a screen that was standing on one side of the room. When she came out a few minutes later she had changed into a long white nightgown with embroidered lace around the bottom. She had undone her hair, which hung nearly to her waist.

Suzy sat down on a chair beside the bed while Grandma organised her pillows. Once settled under the covers, she pointed to something on the other side of the room. 'Fetch me that box on the dresser over there, will you dear?'

Suzy looked around and spotted a small jewellery

box sitting on a lace doily. She picked it up carefully and carried it back to the bed, then handed it to the old lady.

Grandma Phillips looks different with her long white hair hanging down around her shoulders, Suzy thought, as Grandma rummaged through the box and pulled out a red velvet pouch tied with a gold ribbon. She undid the ribbon.

'Here,' she said, holding out her closed hand, 'give me your hand, young lady.'

Suzy reached over and held out her hand. Lovingly, Grandma placed a pendant of silver and turquoise in Suzy's palm. With both her hands she folded Suzy's hand around the piece of jewellery and held them tight.

'Now this is for you, Suzy. I have been waiting a long time to pass this on, but I always knew I would find it a new owner – a beautiful neck for it to hang around, with a beautiful soul to protect. You are now its rightful owner, Suzy; you are the one the pendant has been waiting for – you are a good horsewoman, a lover of horses and you love White Cloud.'

Suzy clasped the gift tightly, hardly daring to open her hand. She felt tears prick the corners of her eyes, and for a moment she didn't know what to say. She felt incredibly honoured.

'Thank you, Grandma . . .' she said hesitantly.

The old lady interrupted her. 'You like being here at White Cloud, don't you Suzy?'

'Yes, I love it, it's, it's just beautiful. So peaceful, and today when I rode up into the hills on Ripple, it kind of felt familiar. It was weird, Grandma.'

'I have the feeling we'll be seeing a lot more of you in the future, out here at White Cloud,' Grandma said with a smile.

Suzy looked down at her clenched fist and slowly released it. There in the palm of her hand was the most beautiful piece of jewellery. She was mesmerised by the colour of the turquoise and the intricately carved detail. She realised she had seen the design somewhere before, but before she had a chance to gather her thoughts Grandma Phillips continued.

'This is the emblem of White Cloud. My mother handed the pendant down to me, and as I had no daughters of my own, nor granddaughters, for that matter, I have been waiting for the right person to give it to. The moment I laid eyes on you I knew . . .' She paused.

'But what about Mike's mother – don't you want to give the necklace to her?' Suzy asked awkwardly. 'Mike never talks about her, and, like, I don't know if she's even . . .'

Grandma frowned. 'We seldom talk about Nicole around here, and when we do, I can tell you it's not favourable.'

'Sorry, Grandma, I didn't mean to pry . . .'

Grandma explained that Nicole had married their son, Calum, and that the two of them had planned to take over White Cloud when Grandad retired. 'Well, not that Hector would ever have fully retired,' she smiled.

'Nicole and Calum were married here at the homestead, and after a few years little Mikey was born. Looking back now, I realise the high country just didn't suit that woman. She liked her expensive designer clothing and city living, and eventually she left her child and husband to move back to the city. Mike was only two years old at the time. Can you imagine that?' Grandma shook her head. 'What sort of mother would leave a toddler?

'So we brought little Mikey up,' she continued with a slight smile. 'That's what we called him when he was a little lad.'

'Cute name . . . but, did she never come back for him?' asked Suzy. 'Didn't she want to have Mike with her?'

'No. She wrote us a letter . . .' Grandma sighed heavily, 'and we took over custody of Mikey.'

'Oh, that's so sad,' Suzy frowned. 'No wonder Mike doesn't talk about her.' She sighed. 'But what about his dad? He never mentions him either.'

'Our son Calum left several years later, when Mike was ten. Calum has remarried and he and his wife now live in Seattle. He used to return to visit Mike in the summer holidays; sometimes Mike would fly over there. Travel was never an issue as Calum is involved with the airlines. He's an airline engineer. He's loved flying all his life. He used to fly top-dressing planes in this area, and he had his own helicopter here at the homestead. He still comes back occasionally, but he's built a new life for himself over there – he's a very busy man these days . . .'

'Wow, that's pretty tough, Grandma,' Suzy said. 'Poor Mike. But I reckon he would have had an awesome time, I mean, growing up with Grandad and you.' She smiled.

'Yes, when Calum decided to move permanently to Seattle, Mike was given the choice of where he wanted to live, but he chose to stay here with us. He's a country boy at heart.'

'I get so tired these days, Suzy. I have to rest now, but before I go to sleep I must tell you about the necklace – it has a special meaning and significance. When my mother gave it to me she told me the turquoise would not only keep me safe around horses but would also keep my horse safe. Tie the pouch onto Ripple if he ever gets ill, and wear the necklace when you are around horses. I always used to wear it when I was with horses.'

'Thank you . . .' Suzy said, then she sat back, letting Grandma Phillips finish what she wanted to say.

'The horses looked after me. Always . . . oh, yes, those precious days with the horses, the smell of the barn, the galloping over the hills . . . I wouldn't have traded that for the world . . .'

As Suzy looked up at Grandma Phillips they both had tears in their eyes..

'Oh Grandma, I don't know what to say. I'm so honoured . . .' Suzy reached forward and hugged the old lady tightly.

'Enough now,' Grandma said abruptly. 'I didn't mean to upset you, child!

'It's funny how people and horses come and go in our lives. Sometimes we have to accept what life throws our way, Suzy. I know about your mother's death, and how much you must miss her. Mike and I have had many conversations about you. He's such a good boy, and tonight when I heard you talking about riding up onto the plateau I knew. I just knew . . .'

'You keep saying that you knew . . . what did you know, Grandma?'

The old lady leant over and put her index finger on Suzy's nose. 'I just know things – that's what. I'm old and wise . . . just like that mare up there . . . Wave – the mare in the mist . . .'

She winked at Suzy, and reached for her hairbrush.

'May I brush your hair, Grandma?'

'Of course, my dear,' she said. 'It's a long time since I had anyone to do that for me.'

As Suzy gently brushed the old lady's hair they talked quietly about their lives. 'You can have anything you want, Suzy,' Grandma said. 'Life is your oyster, you can reach for the stars . . . you can . . .' She closed her eyes and sighed gently. She was tired. She smiled and leant back on her pillows, and said to Suzy, 'Now off you go and join the others downstairs.'

'Sweet dreams. Thank you, Grandma,' whispered Suzy as she turned to leave the room. Glancing back, she saw that the old lady was already asleep. She turned out the light and quietly pulled the big wooden door shut.

She tiptoed down the hallway, trying not to fall off her high heels, and cringed when a loose floorboard creaked under her foot. Again the woman in the painting stared back at her. She leaned over and looked closely at the necklace, then she looked down and opened her hand – it was the same one.

She imagined Grandma riding her hunter, galloping side-saddle and going like the wind. She was gently jolted back to reality by Mike's voice: 'I hope you enjoyed chatting with Grandmother?'

'Oh, yes,' she said as she took Mike's hand. 'She's incredible. What do you know about the turquoise necklace?'

Mike looked up at the portrait of his grandmother. 'It has a lot of meaning, and it's been in the family for a very long time.'

Suzy opened her hand and held it out so that Mike could see the pendant. He whistled quietly.

'Well, all I can say is that Grandma must have a very high opinion of you, Suzy! Come here – I'll do it up for you.'

Suzy handed him the pendant and turned around. Mike fastened it around her neck, then stood back and looked at Suzy, then up at the portrait. He grinned: 'Two pretty cool ladies!

'Now we'd better get to the library!' he said. 'Grandad says he has an important announcement to make!'

He held out his hand to escort Suzy down the stairs. He was pleased that she had shown her respect for his grandparents by changing out of the casual riding clothes she normally wore. And like everyone else in the dining room, he had noticed how pretty she looked.

14

An Important Announcement

When they entered the library, Grandad Phillips was sitting in his silk smoking jacket holding a glass of whisky, with Sam perched up beside him with a hot chocolate.

'Here, sit down, Suzy,' smiled Grandad, pointing to the buttoned leather chair beside him.

'So far so good,' she thought, feeling a little anxious.

Mike sat down next to Sam and put an arm around his shoulders affectionately. 'How are you doing, young Sam – okay? Nearly bedtime; you've had a big day!'

'Sure have,' replied Sam, licking the chocolate from around his lips. 'This farm life sure wears a bloke out!'

Grandad made eye contact with Suzy. 'I've given this a lot of thought, and . . .' he paused. He had on his grumpy face, and Suzy's heart pounded for a moment as she tried to think how she could have upset the old man. Sensing he had pushed her far enough, he smiled and continued, '. . . after watching the way you handle that curly horse of yours, I've made an important decision.' He smiled and took a sip of his Scotch.

Suzy's head didn't turn but her eyes moved left and right to check out Sam and Mike's reactions. Grandad gazed round at each of them in turn, making sure he had their undivided attention, then he stood up to give his words more weight.

'Ripple and Suzy will be joining the round-up of the wild horses this year. It's a four-day trek in and out of the hills – two days out and two days back – but Ripple's fit enough for that, and Suzy, you can obviously handle him well, you're a great little rider. As from this moment you're officially on the team!'

Suzy's jaw dropped. 'But Grandad,' she said, feeling confused, 'I'm not old enough!'

'Phh, what's a year or so. It's not age that's important, it's ability, and you have that! End of discussion. I'm tired – it's time I was in bed. Good night all.' He put his crystal glass on the desk, gathered up his stick and went toward the door. 'Pretty necklace!' he added as he passed Suzy, then before she could reply he was gone.

Suzy was still stunned by Grandad's decision, and Sam was looking equally gobsmacked. Mike looked at them and said, 'Oh well, that's Grandad for you. I need some sleep – catch you guys in the morning. Sam, coming? You can plug your laptop in on the desk here, Suzy, if you want to email the girls. Catch you in the morning – we were talking about having a look at Swan Lake – still on for that?'

'Sounds great. What time shall I set the alarm for?'

'Oh, you won't need an alarm, the birds'll wake you. Good night. And thanks, Suzy, for taking time to chat to Grandmother – I know she'd appreciate it.'

Suzy blushed. 'Well, it was my pleasure. I really enjoyed her company. I forgot she was 89 – for a moment she seemed like one of my own friends.

'And thanks for reminding me, Mike – I told Lucy and Alexa I'd email them tonight. I'll get my laptop. See you guys in the morning.'

Suzy sat in Grandad Phillips' huge buttoned leather

chair, feeling a bit like Goldilocks sitting in Papa Bear's big chair, as the computer made 'trying to connect' noises. The station was too remote to receive wireless, so she had to make do with a slower dial-up connection. She held her breath as she waited for it to connect, desperate to tell the others about Grandad's shock announcement. She still couldn't quite believe it.

Finally the connection was made, and Suzy moved back to the desk to write her email.

Hi Alexa, Lucy

OMG, tonight has been one of the most amazing nights of my life!!!! First, I'm wearing a dress and heels – that for a start is incredibly amazing, right!? LOL.

Secondly, Grandma Phillips gave me the most beautiful turquoise necklace you've ever seen – it's been in their family for years. I can't wait to show you and tell you about its magic. Grandma says it will help keep me safe around horses.

Thirdly – you aren't going to believe this! After dinner Grandad Phillips announced that Ripple and I would be joining in the round-up. I cannnnt wait! Wicked, huh? I'll fill you in more when I have more stuff to pass on to you guys.

Oh, and last but not least, Sam's picked out the most awesome palomino mare. He's been riding her already and he's doing really well. She's quite dark and has big brown eyes that melt your heart.

BTW what have you lot all been up to?

How're the rest of your holidays going? Lucy, how did Hope go at the western show in the weekend? Please email and let me know, I know she would have been the most perfect angel out. And is Mystery still enjoying life with Finn and the other weanlings?

Alexa, how's Liqui going? How are you feeling about the event coming up? Well, this connection is a bit dicky so I'll sign off now in hope that this gets to you both!

Sending you hugs, Suzy

PS Can you please call Dad and tell him my great news! (Not that I wore a dress!) That I'm riding at the round-up!!!!!!!!!!! Yepeeee, yahoo. Second thoughts, knowing Dad, maybe you shouldn't! He'll panic! LOL.

Xox

PPS Hugs to Liqui, Hope, Mystery and Duke. Home soon.

PPPS Big hugs to Dad xox
ooooooooooooooooo

She pressed the 'Send' button and disconnected from the phone line, then she clunked her way, still in her heels, up the stairs toward the guest bedroom. She felt as if she had conquered Everest as she reached the landing and walked along the hallway to her room, this time avoiding the loose floorboard. She swung herself around on one of the bedposts and collapsed flat on her back into what felt like a soft, puffy cloud.

She lay on the softness of the swans'-down quilt and gazed out beyond the open window. She felt grateful she had found a new friend this evening, one who shared and understood her love of horses. She felt grateful too that she was at White Cloud among friends and horses, and she knew that for now this was where she wanted to be most in the world. She thought how her dreams were coming true, and she thought of her mother, then she thought of her father and wondered what he was up to this evening. She admitted to herself that she was missing him. She wished he would find someone special to share his life with and be happy like Grandma and Grandad Phillips were. She hoped he'd like the hugs she'd sent him in the email. One thing she knew for sure was that she had to get her heels off, as her feet had given all they could manage for one night!

She sat up on the edge of the bed and kicked off her shoes, then she placed them neatly beside her riding boots – for a moment she found herself comparing the two completely different styles of footwear. She picked up a boot and held it for a moment. It was scuffed, had flat soles, was comfortable, and best of all it had a little something from the inside of a horse on the heel that smelled familiar. She giggled to herself.

Still euphoric over Grandad's announcement, she skipped barefoot to the open window where she looked out and breathed in the White Cloud air deeply. Grandma's quote jumped into her head, and she declaimed to the horses outside: 'Take the life of cities! Here's the life for me. 'Twere a thousand pities not to gallop free . . .' She looked up to the night sky and the stars above. Thank you, she thought as she reached to them with open arms – thank you!

She looked around at the shapes of the barn and the stables, clearly visible in the moonlight. She wondered if she had woken the horses, and giggled to herself. And then in the silence of the night she listened to the country sounds: an owl calling, the slight snuffling of cattle and horses. Then she glanced up to the night sky again and pulled the window half shut. Too tired to take off the make-up she had put on especially for dinner, she slipped out of her dress and put on her pyjamas, then she collapsed into bed. As she pulled up the cover and her head sank into the soft pillows, she reflected on how relaxed she felt – tonight she felt comforted, she felt protected and she felt *at home*. She was physically tired, but her thoughts were with the old lady. Clutching the necklace that was still hanging around her neck, she drifted off to sleep.

* * *

Just as Mike had predicted, the chorus of birds singing did wake her the following morning. The sun was just rising over the tops of the hills, and a prism of light shining through the leadlight windows hit the edge of her eye. She squinted and sat up in bed, stretching her arms and giving a hearty yawn.

Becoming aware of the pendant hanging around her neck, she put her hand around it and walked to the mirror. She turned this way and that, loving the way the light caught the silver and turquoise as she moved. Then, remembering the emails she had sent the night before, she rushed downstairs to the library to see if anyone had replied.

Hi Suzy

That's so awesome you'll be riding on the round-up!!!!!!!!!!!!!!!!!!!

ARE WE JEALOUS OR WHAT!!!!

Things are ticking along okay here at Jasmine Farm – not nearly as exciting as White Cloud!:(

Hope won the reining pattern so I was rapt! I pulled out of the other classes as I was so pleased with her and decided she'd done enough.

Mystery is enjoying his new life as a big boy! Netty was right, he was ready to leave home. Before I know it he'll be off to boarding school. LOL.

Miss you lots and lots Lucy xox

Hi Suzypu

Liqui is going well and is getting nice and fit. I'm going to the gym now to tone up a bit too ha ha.

Anyhow, we hope to hear from you again soon. Only two more sleeps till the round-up! I bet it's like Christmas when you were a little kid:)) LUCKY YOU!

Hugs Alexa

P.S. Rang up ya Dad and he's great. I didn't mention the round-up though. He'd have a panic attack! !! He'll phone you later in the week about bringing Ripple back here.

Luv us again xox

P.P.S. You may not get us for a few days, something's cropped up, BUT nothing to worry about. Fill you in later.

Luv us for the third time xox

Xx the horses send these to Ripple

Suzy was still trying to figure out the meaning of the last part of Alexa's email as she disconnected the laptop. Suddenly aware that she was still in her pyjamas, she tiptoed out the door, shut it quietly behind her and hurried toward the stairs.

15

Breakfast

Suzy was still wondering about the email and what her friends could possibly be up to as she came back downstairs. She decided not to let it worry her – if it was something serious she knew the girls would have filled her in. She also knew that the written word could be misunderstood. All the same, it was still eating at her. Maybe the girls had found new friends, she wondered uneasily.

She followed the smell of frying bacon, mingled with the aroma of freshly baked bread, to the kitchen, where Cynthia seemed to be juggling a number of things at once.

'Good morning, Suzy,' she said. 'How'd you sleep? Have a seat,' she added, as she took some eggs from a basket.

Suzy wasn't used to being waited on, and she felt a little uncomfortable. 'You seem busy, Cynthia,' she said. 'Would you like me to make omelettes? I'm pretty good at them.'

'Sounds fantastic! The others will be down soon and I'll get the coffee pot organised. You know how Mike loves his brew in the morning!' Cynthia laughed. Suzy could tell she adored Mike.

'Sure do,' she agreed. Then, breaking some eggs into a bowl she went on, 'You must really like it at White Cloud to have lived here for so long.'

'Ron and I adore it. We used to live in the city,

but we couldn't go back now. It's a pretty special way of life here. Besides, we love the Phillips family. They're like our own family.'

'Grandma and Grandad Phillips are pretty amazing all right,' Suzy said as she turned her omelette. 'I guess I'm starting to feel like they're kind of my grandparents too, in a weird sort of way. Like, they don't seem old at all. You can adopt grandparents these days, can't you?'

'Do you not have any grandparents?' Cynthia asked, taking some bread rolls from the oven and putting them on the bench.

'Well, not really. Dad's folks are dead, and my maternal grandparents live in New York. Dad met Mum when he was on holiday there. After they got married they lived there for a while, but I came along yonks later when they'd moved back here. So I don't see them, and I'd really love to . . . it's just that . . .'

Suzy looked down at the omelette and gave it a prod.

'It's just what, sweetheart?' Cynthia asked.

'Well, it's quite complicated really. Since Mum died they've kind of distanced themselves from Dad and me. They don't come and visit any more. Poor Dad, he can't really understand it. They say it's too painful for them since my Mum died. I don't really understand it either, but I guess I just have to accept that's the way they are. Dad's not too happy with them, but there's not much he can do about the situation – he has enough to deal with. He has a million patients all needing his attention, but he does say it's not fair on me. It's my dream, yet another dream of mine, to see them again. One day.'

'Oh, that is sad, Suzy. Well, I think we'd better see if Grandma and Grandad Phillips want an adoptive grand-daughter, huh?' She gave Suzy's shoulder a slight squeeze.

Suzy smiled. She kind of liked Cynthia's suggestion. 'You don't think Grandad Phillips is a bit grumpy though, do you?'

'No, not really. He's a very kind man, although I must admit he changed a bit after he stopped riding. He lost a bit of his sparkle. Grandma and horses were the passions in his life – ha, and good Scotch, of course. No, seriously – horses were his life. When you take a person's passion away you destroy their soul. He's got a heart condition, you know, and the doctor thinks it's too risky for him to ride, but the thing is – his heart is breaking – and only the horses will mend it, in my opinion.'

Cynthia started lining up plates on the bench, ready for portions of bacon and Suzy's omelette.

'Anyway, one day you will see your grandparents again. If that's your dream, Suzy, make it happen. It's only an aeroplane ride away!'

'Yeah, I have actually thought about going over to see them! I have to save some money, though. Don't say anything to Sam,' she whispered as she heard footsteps approaching, 'but it'll take all my savings to buy Bubbles for him.'

Sam bounded into the room cheerfully, looking rather like a junior cowboy. It was obvious that Mike was quickly becoming his idol, and Sam was copying some of his style. He sat down and rounded his eyes in the direction of the food.

'Good morning, Sam, how did you sleep?' Suzy wondered if this was how Cynthia greeted everyone in the mornings.

'I slept really well, thanks. But I've been up for ages. I rode Bubbles to the gate and cleared the box!' He put a pile of mail on the table.

'Sam, are you interested in going to Swan Lake?' Suzy asked as Cynthia passed him a plate of food.

'You're kidding me, aren't you?' Sam cringed, wondering why on earth Suzy would want to take him to a ballet. 'Err, I'm really not into that dancing stuff!'

The women hooted with laughter. 'No, Sam, Swan Lake at Lake Ridge, here on the station. Mike and I are riding out to see the wild swans.'

'Wow, can I ride Bubbles there?'

'You'll have to check with Mike on that one. He's the boss when it comes to Bubbles and you.'

'Yes, you can take Bubbles, Sam,' Mike announced, walking in and heading for the coffee pot. With coffee in hand he walked back to the table, where he flicked through the pile of mail. Then he saw it. The envelope was addressed to Mr Michael Phillips, and a logo on the front showed it was from the Veterinary College.

Mike ripped open the envelope and unfolded the letter that was inside. He read it quickly, knowing it could change his whole future.

'Yes!' he yelled, punching the air, the letter still gripped in his hand. 'Yes, yes, yes!' He thumped the table with his fists. The cutlery bounced and the coffee spilt, none of which Mike noticed. He looked up, grinning from ear to ear, then he reached over and grabbed Suzy. Squeezing her arms, he looked into her eyes. 'I've been accepted for Vet College!'

'Mike!' Suzy gasped. 'Wow! That's fantastic news! Congratulations!'

'Well, this is cause for a celebration!' said Cynthia, who loved any opportunity for a party.

'Yep, more golden champagne bubbles!' Sam joined in.

'Excuse me all, I have to find Grandma and Grandad!' Mike interrupted, giving the wall a friendly thump as he quickly left the kitchen. 'Yes, yes, yessss! And I should just fit in a quick trip to Virginia before I start university! Yesss, it's all good.'

The room was suddenly quiet, then Mike popped his head back around the corner, a mischievous grin of his face. 'Oh by the way, meet you guys saddled up at the barn ready to go at nine. Be ready to roll – it'll take us 45 minutes to ride to Swan Lake. Remember to take the packed lunches our lovely Cynthia has kindly made up for you.'

He disappeared again, and they heard his footsteps fading as he hoofed it along the corridor.

16

Swan Lake

The sun was shining down on Suzy and Sam as they waited, with their saddled-up horses, at the barn. Suzy was wondering how Grandma and Grandad had taken Mike's news. It was sooo exciting. At the same time, as she looked up at the hills she couldn't help feeling tingly inside thinking about the coming round-up.

'You'll have to hold the fort back here while we're on the round-up, Sam. You'll look after Grandma and Grandad Phillips, eh?'

'Sure will,' Sam nodded. 'I'm good at cutting firewood, collecting eggs from the chickens, checking that the troughs have enough water, feeding the horses at night and . . .'

There was no doubt about it – he was indispensable. Suzy chuckled quietly, wondering how White Cloud had survived so long without him.

'I guess you won't want to go back to boarding school, huh?'

'Mmm, not much choice really. Anyhow, it'll be better this year cos I'll have Bubbles!' Sam replied, hugging his horse.

'Well, you're lucky. Not everyone gets to take a horse to school!' Suzy smiled.

'Yeah, I am – thanks to you! It's fun here, eh Suzy?

I love it, you know, with all the horses around us.'

'Well, Sam, just wait till we arrive back with the wild horses – you ain't seen nothin' yet!'

'Yeah, can't wait, can we Bubbles!'

'You know Bubbles used to be one of them,' Suzy told him. 'I remember meeting her here last year when she was brought down from the hills.'

'D'you think she misses her mum and her horse family? D'you think she'll recognise her mother if she comes in with the wild herd?'

'I don't know if she misses her mum – I guess she's adjusted in a way. Besides, she has you now, Sam. And yes, I think she'll recognise her horse family if they come down with the herd.'

'But that might not be good – she might want to go back with them.'

'No she won't, Sam; she loves you now, you're her family. Anyway, if she was still in the wild at her age, she would probably have joined another band of horses by now.'

'You reckon?' Sam said slightly anxiously. 'You're not just saying that to make me feel better?'

'No,' Suzy laughed. 'I wouldn't lie to you. You're my hero, remember, and you kind of feel like family – hey, I don't see why we can't form our own family just like the horses do.'

'Yeah, I can still have Uncle George and Aunty Kate as my *other* family, but you and Ripple and Mike and Flair and Lucy and Hope and Alexa and Liquorice and Grandma and Grandad Phillips and . . . um, that's all . . . you'll be my *horse* family. Oh and I'll include Cynthia, because she's really good at cooking and I love her baked potatoes.' He giggled. 'They can all be the White Cloud Family.'

'You're a hard shot,' Suzy told him. 'Sounds excellent to me – Mr Samuel White-Cloud and Mrs Champagne Bubbles White-Cloud.'

Just as they had finished sorting out their new family, Mike cantered up on Flair.

'Right, you lot ready to go? Sorry it took a bit longer than expected. Grandad wanted to talk about my becoming a vet. It kind of doesn't match exactly with his plans for me to run White Cloud Station later on . . .' Mike was a little solemn. 'You know I wouldn't break that old man's heart for the world.'

* * *

They set off, at first taking the same route that Suzy and Ripple had taken on their earlier adventure into the mountains. But instead of continuing on to the eastern plateau they turned to the west at the giant rock she remembered passing, and climbed higher into the hills. It was quite a steep climb, and the track was too narrow to trot along safely. Mike was pretty cautious, not wanting to put Suzy and Sam, or the horses, at risk.

'We'll give the horses a quick break here,' he suggested after they had climbed up a fair way. 'This is called Frog Face Rock – take a look, Sam. Can you see the formation of a frog's face in the rock above?'

'Awesome,' replied Sam.

After a five-minute rest and a drink from their water bottles, they mounted their horses again and continued down a winding track. Past Frog Face Rock it became rockier, and white and pink foxgloves edged the riding track. The formation of the land changed slightly, and giant boulders dotted the landscape. As they wound their way down among the boulders the wildflowers bounced back and forward against their stirrups. When the land opened up again it was more rolling, with spectacular views and a backdrop of hills, woven together by white clouds. The shallow edges of the lake provided a haven for large numbers of birds and other wildlife. Suzy was amazed at the variety, but what caught her eye the most were the wild swans.

'This, my friends, is Swan Lake!' Mike stated grandly.

'This is amazing!' Suzy replied.

'Are there any lizards?'

'Could be, Sam, since they're out sunning themselves during the day, but they're hard to catch.'

'Oh yeah, they're nockchurnal.'

'Nocturnal, Sam,' Mike nodded. 'Right then, let's give these horses a rest, guys.'

'This must be one of the most beautiful places I've ever seen,' Suzy exclaimed as she dismounted, ran up her stirrups and loosened Ripple's girth strap. 'Mike, this is awesome!'

With the horses unsaddled and nibbling happily on the rough grass they sat beside the lake and watched the swans and their babies. Mike pointed out the different birds and plants to Suzy as they sat and chatted.

'What do you *want* to do, Mike?' Suzy asked suddenly, as she picked some wild daisies to finish the chain she had been making. 'Do you want to go away and become a vet, or do you want to stay and run White Cloud and be with the horses?'

Mike thought for a while. 'I want to make Grandad happy, and I want to work with horses. I *have* to be with horses, Suzy, and I want to be a vet.'

'Then you must tell Grandad,' Suzy replied seriously, putting the daisy chain on her head. 'He'll understand. My mother once said to me, "You must do what's good for your soul." I didn't really understand then, as I was quite young, but I'm beginning to. I think horses are good for my soul – I think I need to be around horses too.'

'Me too!' Sam piped up. 'They just make me feel real good inside! They smell good too, and they look good and they can carry you to faraway places like right here at Swan Lake. I think they must be in my blood too, cos I really love them!'

'That kid! He has a knack of making the conversation lighter when it's getting too deep and meaningful,' Mike laughed. 'Hey Sam,' he said, pointing to the lake, 'why don't you see if you can see any fish down there? It's quite difficult sometimes, Suzy,' he said. 'I want to go away, I want to go and learn how to become a vet and study horses, and I want to be with Grandma and Grandad – and I kind of like being around you guys too. Is it so bad to want so many things?'

'It's wonderful, Mike. It's very cool to have ambition and choices. It will all become clear. Maybe four days in the mountains will do you good!'

'Sure, nothin' like good country air to clear the old brain cells,' Sam chipped in. 'Imagine if Grandad could ride again. That might make him less sad about you going away and leaving him; maybe he needs something nice as well as sad?'

'Of course! You're a genius, Sam. Grandad needs to get back in the saddle again! Out of the mouths of babes!' Mike exclaimed. He sighed and lay back in the grass, looking up at the blue sky above.

'I ain't a babe! Suzy's a babe, eh Mike?' Sam piped up.

'Sam, you're embarrassing me!' Suzy laughed,

burying her face in her hands.

'I'm going to see if there're any fish in this lake!' Sam announced, oblivious to Suzy's confusion.

'Yes, I think you'd better disappear!' Suzy replied, still not wanting to show her face.

'Good idea, Sam!' Mike laughed. 'Before I get up and throw you in!'

Sam ran towards the lake, laughing. 'Can you keep an eye on Bubbles?'

'Is that one happy kid, or what?' asked Mike.

'Who wouldn't be happy up here at White Cloud? Oops sorry, not timely, when you're thinking of going away to uni. It's just that it's kind of special here, Mike. Riding out here gives me such a feeling of freedom. Money can't buy the freedom a horse gives me. And this huge open space feels like it goes on and on forever. Dad's apartment in town is so very different to here. I love everything about this place – the smell of horses, the wildflowers and the birds calling. It's truly awesome! Know what I mean?'

'Of course I do, Suzy. And can you imagine what it's been like for Grandad not being able to come up here for a ride? He always loved riding out here to the lake and up to Koru Falls; there are some pretty magical spots in these hills. He hasn't been the same since the doctor told him he's not to get on the back of a horse again. The doctor thinks it would put too much strain on his heart. They treat him like a frail old man who's going to break! But he's ridden for years, and he's riding fit still. I mean, what's the worst that could happen?'

Suzy patted the ground beside her as Sam panted up to them. 'Well I suppose the worst thing that could happen is that he'd have a fall. And, with all due respect to my dad, my mum used to say, "Doctors don't always know what's best for the soul –sometimes you need a bit of magic." I'll never forget the times when I was quite young and sick – I'd have quite bad bouts of asthma and stuff, and she'd wrap me in a blanket and drive me out to Riverbed Flats where there was a herd of horses. They'd gallop around the huge open river flats. We called them the magic horses – I'm not really sure whether they were wild or not, but they sure seemed it. I think they were probably retired and broken-down racehorses,' she added, giggling tenderly. 'Whatever they were, they had their own magical aura. It was very special, a bit like this place. It was only a small herd, nothing like the herds of White Cloud. Mum would say, "Look at the wild horses, Suzy, breathe in the magic of the horses, and they'll make you better!"'

Suzy sat up and breathed in the air, just as she had back then. 'I could see little horses floating all around me. I called them the magic horse fairies, and I would take my hands from under the blanket and I would grab at the air and grab the horse fairies. I would reach and grab and reach and grab and giggle and, miraculously, I would begin to feel better. When I had them safely in my hands I would put them in the pockets of my jacket, and then my pants pockets, and I'd take them home. And just in case there were any still floating about, I'd breathe in some more. I mean normal breathing was difficult, let alone breathing in something the size of a healing horse fairy!' She laughed. 'Is this a silly story for guys to hear?'

'It's amazing!' Sam told her. 'Did they make you all better?'

'Mum and I would sit there for what seemed like eternity, and we would watch them graze, gallop and play. It was "our secret", and we never told Dad when we'd been to the river flats. He wouldn't have been very happy – he always thought of me as fragile. Mum would put her finger on her lips to remind me not to say anything to Dad when he would comment a day or two later how much better I was. Every time this happened I would say, "It must be your good medicine, Daddy!" But I knew, even at that age, that it was the magic of horses that made me feel better and lifted my spirits.'

She paused and looked out over at the swans, then

she smiled. 'As I get older I'll grow out of my asthma, but I'll never grow out of the magic of horses. I don't have half as many health problems now, and Dad's medicine does help when I have a reaction or attack – I wouldn't be without my inhaler, but I wouldn't be without horses either! Hopefully by the time I'm about 20 or so I'll be over it, huh?'

'Yeah, hope so,' Mike said. 'It's good you've got Ripple anyway.

'That story about your mother taking you to the wild horses was amazing. You don't ever forget experiences like that. She was right, too – the horses did help you, even if it was from a distance!' Mike smiled.

'Yeah,' Sam piped up. With his serious face on he continued, 'Bubbles is magic too, and sooo healing for me. I'm off to check again for fish to catch!'

'I'm so lucky that I found out about the curly breed,' Suzy sighed. 'I was at my wits' end, thinking I wouldn't be able to follow my passion. I just can't imagine not having horses in my life! I know I've been so much happier – well, not that I was unhappy – but I'm *extra* happy now that I've got Ripple around me most of the time – he's good for my soul.'

'Yes, I agree about what's good for the soul. Getting back to the "Grandad Plan", I think it's unlikely he would fall off a horse – he's brilliant in the saddle. He just needs one special, kind of steady and trustworthy horse that will really look after him. We're going to need a pretty magic kind of horse.'

Suzy turned around and pointed to Ripple. 'Well then – there he is – what are we waiting for?'

17

The Plan

Sam didn't see any fish. He lay down on his stomach beside Suzy and Mike and looked out over the lake. Then he looked over at the horses, who were grazing contentedly on an assortment of weeds and grasses, and pulling the seed heads off the grass.

'Whatcha been talking about?' he asked.

'Well, actually, we've been discussing how great it would be to see Grandad on a horse again, on the back of Ripple,' said Suzy. 'So, we need a plan!'

'We just have to figure out how to get him onto Ripple,' Mike added, rubbing his brow and hair with one hand and holding his cowboy hat in the other.

'I know, I know, here's a good idea,' Sam interrupted. 'I saw this TV programme once about a guy in a wheelchair. He couldn't walk by himself, so he taught his horse to lie down on the ground, and he brought his wheelchair right up beside the horse, and from his wheelchair he pulled himself onto his horse's back. Amazzzing, it was! And then he taught his mate's horse to do the same, so the two guys could go riding together. It was very cool!'

'Wow!' said Suzy. 'That is cool!'

'Yep, it was awesome the way the horses just got up

once these guys were on them, and off they went. They said it made them feel good. I thought it was cool because those guys had legs that could walk again! Pretty amazing stuff.'

'Yes, that's a pretty neat story, Sam,' Mike said thoughtfully. 'It's a possibility.'

'What is?' asked Suzy. 'Do you mean teaching Ripple to lie down?'

'The only trouble is, it's something only an experienced horseman should do –'

'Well, you're experienced!' Suzy interrupted.

'It's not that,' Mike replied. 'It's just that it can take time to teach something like that. Some horses learn really quickly and others don't like it all.'

'Oh, I see,' replied Suzy.

'Besides, it would be really cool to do it now. I mean before the round-up, don't you agree?'

'Yeah,' replied Sam, 'like today!'

'Today?!' exclaimed Suzy.

'Well, why not?' asked Mike.

'No reason when I think about it!' Suzy replied. She took a deep breath and sighed loudly. 'Right then, we need a Plan B!'

'Well,' Sam said, in an authoritative voice, 'Uncle George has a truck at home and it has this hoist on the back. He lifts everything and anything, man! Get it – man?' He giggled.

'Are you saying we should hoist Grandad into the air,' Mike said with a huge smile on his face, trying not to laugh, 'on the back of Ron's truck?'

'Like think about it! I mean, we could lift him up and lower him down onto Ripple! It's quite simple really if you think about it!' To Sam the idea was completely logical.

Mike and Suzy fell about at the idea, and Suzy said with a gasp, 'I can just see Grandad Phillips swinging around in midair by his pants' belt, yelling "Get me down!" and Ripple having fifty fits at the unidentified flying object hovering above him – flying above him like one of those nectar-filled wood pigeons coming in to land! Whompha crasssh bang, here comes Grandad in for landing. Are your wheels down?' Suzy was hitting her stride now. 'And he's flapping about up there – he scares Ripple, who honks – you know, that special honk to warn the other horses of danger – and before you know it he's bolted off at full tilt, galloping into the sunset.' She fell back into the grass, clutching her sides.

'Yeah!' Now it was Mike's turn. 'And poor old Grandad is swinging round and round in the air getting all red in the face and waving his fist. Yelling, "Get me down!" Oh hell, that's the last thing his dicky ticker needs!'

'Yeah,' Sam added gleefully, 'and screaming, "I'll have your guts for garters when I get down!"'

Now they were all rolling on their backs in the grass and hooting into the blue sky above. It was the funniest thing they'd heard in a long time – the thought of Grandad Phillips swaying in the breeze and Ripple bolting out the gate, then everyone running after Ripple and leaving Grandad swinging like a kite in the wind – and all because of their good intentions of getting the old horseman back where he belonged, on the back of a horse.

'Ouch, my stomach hurts, I'm laughing so much,' Suzy managed to blurt out, 'Ooouch!'

'Me too,' laughed Sam.

Mike couldn't even manage any words, he was laughing so much.

* * *

'That was such cool fun,' Sam said enthusiastically as they turned in at the gates to the homestead. 'Thank you so much, Mike.' He leant over and patted Bubbles on the neck. 'And you too, Bubbles; thank you for taking me up to Swan Lake. Oh, and thanks Suzy and Ripple and Flair for your company.'

As they walked their horses up the long driveway Suzy kept thinking of the exciting days to come – the thunder of hooves, the dust, the wild horses heading toward the yards, and then finally the auction. She gathered up Ripple's reins, noticing how keen he was to get back to his grassy paddock. 'Is it sometimes difficult, Mike?' she asked thoughtfully. 'Like, you know, watching the horses go to new homes?'

Mike thought for a moment before answering.

'Well, as you know, Suzy, we check out all the potential buyers before the auction. There's *no way* our horses go to homes we don't approve of. It's not fair for wild horses to end up with just anyone. I've seen it before in other areas – just because people have money to buy a horse it doesn't mean they have good horsemanship skills. Our horses *have* to go to experienced people – people who *know* about horses – and not to people who can only *afford* them.'

'I know,' Suzy agreed. 'I've seen that happen too. I reckon the best way to learn good horse handling and riding skills is from old guys like Grandad. You can't tell me that all those years, day in, day out in their company, don't add up to something.'

'Well, it's not just years, Suzy; it's how open you are. Being a good horseman is not just about horses.'

Suzy was a little puzzled at Mike's statement. I'll figure this out later, she thought to herself.

* * *

With the horses untacked and tied to the washing bay Suzy looked at Mike, 'So do we do it then?'

'You're serious, aren't you?'

'Sure am. Why not? It'd be too awkward trying to get him on a horse any other way.'

'I've got a better idea,' Mike began to laugh, reliving the vision of 'the flying grandfather'. 'The cattle race! I'll finish hosing Flair, dry her off and then we'll get

Ripple lined up by the cattle race. We'll get him to stand there, and Ron and I can help lower Grandad down from the platform onto Ripple's back. With Ripple standing steady, and Ron and I on either side, it'll work. I'll talk to Ron at afternoon break and we'll work it around Ron's schedule. Ripple will be refreshed by then. Can you have him saddled up and over by the loading ramp at 3.30?'

'Done deal.'

'Oh, and you'll find a western saddle in the tack room. It has Grandad's initials in silver engraving on the side – you can't miss it. Put that on Ripple, Suzy, please.'

18

Back in the Saddle

Afternoon tea was always delicious at White Cloud. Cynthia's hot scones, covered in cream and home-made raspberry jam, always ensured everyone arrived on the porch on time.

'C'mon, Sam, we'd better get Ripple spruced up. Thanks for the delicious scones, Cynthia,' Suzy said as she nodded at Sam to move. Sam grabbed another scone from the plate, quickly thanked Cynthia, and walked off beside Suzy.

Maybe the time was right, maybe the old man's heart really was breaking because he had been missing his riding – whatever the reason, it seemed Grandad hadn't needed much persuading.

'Ya know what,' Sam said seriously, scoffing his scone. 'I reckon this is such a cool idea. But I'm a bit worried – Grandad won't break any bones, will he?'

'No, you heard what Mike said – it's unlikely he'll fall off. I mean, like once you've learnt how to ride you never forget!' Suzy reassured him.

Meanwhile Ron and Mike had hopped on the four-wheeler and headed down to the cattle yards. They had a few minor adjustments to make in preparation for Grandad Phillips' ride.

Suzy caught Ripple while Sam went into the barn

and collected the grooming kit and hoof oil.

'What bridle do you want?' he called from inside the tack room.

'You'd better use the bridle that's hanging beside Grandad's saddle, Sam. And the turquoise saddle cloth.'

Sam came out, staggering slightly under the big saddle. 'Gee, this is a mighty big fancy saddle!' Puffing, he placed the saddle on the ground beside Suzy as she brushed Ripple's mane. Then, as she continued brushing Ripple all over, he picked up the hoof pick and started to clean Ripple's hooves out.

'Tell you what, Sam, why don't you saddle up Bubbles? Maybe Grandad would like to ride with you!'

'Cool,' Sam beamed, quickly turning to collect Bubbles' gear. 'That's an awesome idea!'

* * *

By the time Suzy had finished with him Ripple was gleaming, and his ears pricked as he paraded Grandad's fine saddlery to the cattle yards. Suzy felt proud of the way she was presenting her horse for such a momentous occasion. Bubbles and Sam followed behind, Sam sitting tall and proud as they approached the yards.

Grandad Phillips was on the left side of the race beside Mike, while Ron was on the other side.

'Now what I want you to do, Suzy, is to lead Ripple through this gap and stand him right here,' Mike said, pointing out the spot. Grandad Phillips watched from the platform. He was dressed in his blue shirt, his Wrangler jeans that Mike had brought back from Virginia, and his black stetson. He looked so smart you'd have thought he was off to a rodeo.

 Suzy followed Mike's instructions precisely and halted Ripple directly beside the platform.

'Now, make sure he stands still, Suzy.'

'Yep, will do. Whoaaa Ripple, standddd,' she whispered soothingly, stroking Ripple's neck. 'Good boy.'

Ripple wasn't at all perturbed by the goings on, standing calmly as Grandad was lowered into the saddle with the support of the two strong men.

There was silence, as if the whole world had stopped, and the old man smiled as tears rolled down his cheeks. 'It's been too long, lad, far too long!' He looked up at Mike on the platform, then continued gruffly, 'Doesn't do for a man to behave this way!'

'I know, Grandad,' Mike swallowed hard and smiled gently. 'I know, but us fellas are allowed to cry too, you know.'

Grandad returned the smile and time stood still – Ripple stood quietly while everyone enjoyed the moment.

'Ready?' asked Suzy, turning to check on Grandad as she prepared to lead Ripple out of the race.

'Of course I'm ready, lass! Now you undo that damned lead rope. I might be old but I'm not dopey!'

Grandad Phillips gathered up the reins and jogged Ripple into the open space beside the cattle yards, then he took him through a range of movements, to which Ripple responded with precision.

'Wow, I haven't taught him any of those,' Suzy exclaimed, impressed.

'It's all the same work – all the basics that we've done with him build up to those. Besides, that's no ordinary rider on board! That's Grandad!' Mike laughed.

Grandad asked Ripple to canter to the right, he took the right lead, then he did a circle of his imaginary arena and came across the diagonal and asked Ripple to change to the left. Ripple did a perfect flying change midair. 'You're a smart horse,' the old man whispered, smiling.

Suzy was amazed. Grandad looked just like Mike riding. He was a natural in the saddle. He was home!

Grandad sat upright in the saddle, without touching

the reins, and stopped Ripple in front of them. Turning to Sam, he asked, 'Ready, boy?'

Sam took up his reins. 'Um, yes, but what for exactly, Grandad?'

'For a bloody good gallop!' Grandad Phillips replied with a mischievous grin.

At that the two riders headed out of the cattle yards toward the homestead. At a steady-in-hand gallop they went up the rose-lined driveway to the main entrance of the house, where Grandma Phillips was sitting doing some crochet.

'Oh my dear lord!' She dropped her crochet and rose up out of her chair, helped by Cynthia, who had been sitting beside her reading in the shade of the veranda. Grandad and Sam did a lap of honour in front of the two women, then like a couple of cowboys from a Wild West movie they pulled their horses up in front of them.

'Oh my gawd! Help me down to the men,' Grandma exclaimed, beaming.

Sam and Grandad sat on their horses smiling, their horses panting.

'You wait there, my darling,' Grandad called, signalling her to stop. 'I'll bring him up the steps.'

'Yep, he's good at steps, Grandad; remember we told you about how he climbed all the way up the steps at Castle Point.'

Ripple followed his rider's lead and climbed the stone steps onto the veranda. His hooves made a hollow noise as he walked along the large cemented stones.

Cynthia supported Grandma Phillips as she walked toward Ripple, took Grandad's hand, and spoke quietly through her tears. 'My darling, it's so very good to see you smile again! And it's been a long time since I've seen that sparkle in your eyes!'

They squeezed each other's hands tightly and smiled into each other's eyes. Ripple stood motionless – he always knew.

'Yes, just what the doctor ordered!' Grandad agreed, nodding his head.

'Not!' Sam piped up from his place on Bubbles, who was standing on the front lawn in front of an array of roses.

'Let go of my arm, Cynthia,' Grandma Phillips commanded, pulling away. She reached up and cradled her arms around Ripple's neck, then she buried her face in his curly mane and kissed him several times. 'Thank you, Ripple,' she whispered, 'for bringing my man back to me,' and she looked up through her teary eyes, patted her husband on the arm, and smiled. 'You take the horses back now, dear, and don't go leading young Sam astray.'

Sam laughed out loud. 'Grandad?'

'Oh Sam, I could tell you some stories about Grandad!'

Grandad Phillips turned Ripple on his haunches and they climbed down the steps to the path. Ripple couldn't resist reaching out and pulling a rose from the nearest bush.

'Ready, boy?'

'Yep – for what exactly, Grandad?'

'Race you to the iron gates!'

Grandma Phillips watched as they cantered off. 'Now isn't that a sight? Now isn't that a *beautiful* sight. I'd go happy with that on my mind if I passed away tonight.' She nodded to Cynthia. 'A palomino and a bay curly horse – a young boy and an old man.'

She paused, watching as they cantered down the drive. Then she breathed in and held her head high: 'Horses lend us the wings we lack.'

The two cowboys slowed to a walk as they neared the cattle yards.

'We'd better act our ages, huh Sam?' winked Grandad Phillips.

'Sure thing,' Sam winked back, not quite as successfully as Grandad. 'Wouldn't do for the others to think we're irresponsible with our horses, would it?'

* * *

As Suzy was about to lead Ripple back to the barn, she stopped suddenly. 'Oh, one more thing, Grandad,' she said, pulling her iPod out of her pocket. 'Here, I've recorded some nice blues for you – Mike told me you loved the blues.'

She leant over and placed the earphones in his ears and turned up the volume. Grandad beamed and yelled above the music, thinking no one could hear him. 'Well, isn't this grand! Thank you, Suzy.' He pulled the earphones out of his ears and went to hand the iPod back to Suzy.

'Oh no, Grandad, it's for you. My gift to you.'

'For me? My own yPod. Well, isn't technology great! Thank you, lass.' He laughed as he walked off, this time with a bounce in his bandy legs and the iPod firmly around his neck.

'I haven't seen Grandad like that for a long time!' laughed Mike. 'Thanks, Suzy, for lending him your horse.'

'Well, I guess what goes around comes around! You know – the black hat brigade!' she replied, remembering again Mike and Grandad's kindness in sending Ripple to her. 'Anyhow, it's Ripple who should be thanked – he really looked after Grandad. Horses just know, don't they!'

Mike smiled. 'They are very intelligent creatures, all right!'

19

Unexpected Visitors

After the excitement of Grandad Phillips' ride, Suzy's emotions were mixed. She felt proud of the part she and Ripple had played in getting Grandad on horseback again, but she now had to focus on what came next. It was all happening, and the tranquillity she had felt was being overridden by the thrill of being involved in the round-up. At the same time, she was also looking forward to returning to Jasmine Farm and eventing soon.

She hadn't planned on being at the auction this year, and never in her wildest dreams had she imagined she would be part of the round-up team. It was exhilarating to be on the other side of the fence – to be one of the riders! She was sorry Lucy and Alexa would not be part of it too, though she knew they wouldn't really be jealous. They were teasing, she thought. All the same, it would have been perfect if they could have been there too.

She wasn't sure if she would be able to eat much dinner that night. The butterflies had returned; the excitement of the next day was getting to her already, and she had an afternoon and a night to get through. She led Ripple to the blacksmith shop, where Mike was hot-shoeing Flair. The mare didn't seem at all disturbed by the steam that hissed around her as Mike moulded a shoe on her hoof then dipped it into the bucket of cold water. He hung the shoe on the side of the bucket then fitted the next one.

'I'll check Ripple for you next, Suzy; just tie him up to the hitching rail. I won't be long.'

'It's okay,' Suzy replied. 'I'll watch if you don't mind. I haven't really seen hot-shoeing before. The Jasmine Farm farrier uses pre-made shoes and shapes them on the anvil without heating them.'

'We've always done it this way here – hot-shoeing, I mean. Grandad used to shoe all the horses himself. He'd even forge his own steel to make all the shoes. He reckons you get a better fit this way – he says it's a science all of its own. I don't recall him ever pricking a hoof or having a horse go lame from bad workmanship. Not a bad record, huh?'

As he cooled off Flair's final shoe, he asked, 'Now, do you reckon we can leave this horse of yours barefoot?'

'Well, I'd quite like it if we can. We haven't had any problems so far – what do you reckon?'

'He sure has tough little feet,' Mike said. 'His hooves are as hard as stone. Most of the riding is on grass so he should be fine,' he added, examining one of Ripple's hooves. 'You might want shoes on him if you go eventing though. If fact you might need studs if the going is a bit slippery. But we'll check that out closer to the event.'

Mike lifted up each of Ripple's hooves in turn, examining and rasping each one. 'Looks like there are a few folk arriving already,' he commented. 'You'd remember how the paddocks fill up with tents, campers and trucks as it gets closer to the auction.

'We'll get away early in the morning. Most of the round-up crew are here already, I think. There're only a couple more to arrive, and then it'll be action stations.'

'I'm so excited,' Suzy said, her voice a bit shaky. 'I can't wait! It's been such an amazing day! I don't know if I can stand it! Not much more could happen in one day.'

Mike smiled. 'I'll just finish shoeing Flair then I'll go and get these visitors sorted.'

'You need a hand, Mike?' Suzy asked, slightly confused. She couldn't quite work out his smile.

'Tell you what – why don't you go and see if the guys camping need anything. There are extra supplies at the house – they might want some milk or eggs, stuff like that.'

'I'll just put Ripple back in his paddock, then I'll go and check on them,' Suzy replied. 'C'mon, Ripple.'

She led the horse back down past the barn and through the campers' paddock to his own, then she bolted the gate, stroked his nose, and gave him a piece of carrot from her pocket. After she had hung up his halter she walked back to the campers' paddock. Despite her earlier fears about dinner she was actually starting to feel a bit hungry, so she took another piece of carrot from her pocket and bit into it. She was looking forward to some of Cynthia's salad for lunch – she had seen her picking lettuces earlier in the day.

But first she had a few chores to attend to. She started with the campervans, knocking on the doors, introducing herself and making a list of requests. Most of them were well organised, so she went on to the few tents that had been erected. She missed the girls more than ever now – the tents reminded her of how they had camped together the previous year.

'Hmm, excuse me,' she said tentatively, leaning down to a tent door that was zipped closed. 'I'm Suzy – I'm just doing the rounds to make sure you're okay – is there anything you need?'

'Ohhh yesss,' a croaky old voice wafted out. 'We'll be wanting a roast dinner at six, accompanied by a bottle of wine. Delivered to the tent, please, dearest.'

Suzy put her hand over her mouth in amazement. How on earth did she handle this! Were they serious?

The elderly voice continued from inside the tent,

'... and we'll be needing some nice soft, scented toilet paper ... and ... SURPRISE!'

The tent flap unzipped and out popped two familiar faces!

'Surprise, dearest!' shrieked Alexa, still in her old lady's voice, as she hugged Suzy. 'Did I have you fooled?'

'I'll, I'll ...' Suzy was speechless.

'Did we trick you?' Lucy asked, reaching out to hug Suzy.

Suzy burst out laughing, and the three of them shrieked as they hugged one another.

'What on earth?' Suzy demanded. 'What on earth are you doing here? That email! Were you planning to surprise me?'

'Yes! Mike and Sam rang us, they organised it. They reckoned you were missing us, and Mike suggested it would be a fantastic finish to the summer holidays.'

'But the best part's still to come!' Alexa blurted out.

'What could be better than this?' Suzy replied, hugging a friend on each side. 'Unexpected campers!'

20

Happiness

'If you look over there you'll see our coach,' Lucy told Suzy. 'My folks drove up. C'mon over and see them on your rounds.'

'Cool, it'll be great to catch up with Dawn and Joe.'

They walked over to the coach and climbed into the living area, where Dawn and Joe were sitting with Suzy's father.

'Oh, Dad, you made it on time this year! NOT that you will have to buy a curly horse or anything,' Suzy said jokingly, hugging her father. 'But I can't wait for you to see Sam riding his new palomino. He's called her Champagne Bubbles.'

'I look forward to meeting Champagne Bubbles! It's so good to see you, Suzy,' her father replied, hugging her fiercely. 'Over dinner I want to hear all about your stay at White Cloud – and how your health has been.'

'It's been so cool, and my health's been fine. I'd better go finish my chores right now, and tell Cynthia not to worry about me for dinner – shall I come back down here, say around six-ish?'

'We'll see you up at the big house later on,' replied her father. 'We're all invited up there for a barbecue tonight. Apparently Mike and Sam are doing the cooking.' He turned toward Lucy and Alexa. 'Are you girls going to tell Suzy your news now, or shall we make her wait until later?' he teased.

'Daaddd!' Suddenly Suzy felt as if she was about five

years old and about to have a major tantrum. 'Tell me, tell me!'

'Oh, all right then – the surprise is around there,' Lucy said, nodding in the direction of the side of the compartment. 'Take a peek around the side.'

Suzy opened the door to the horse compartment and went through. It had been recently washed out, but it still smelt of horses and that lingering fresh-manure smell that never worried her – it was all part of the delicious horse bouquet. She clambered down the back ramp, swinging off the side wall to see what the mystery was. There, to her huge surprise, were Liquorice and Hope, tied up and chomping happily on their hay-nets. They both stopped eating momentarily, startled at Suzy's sudden appearance.

'I knew I smelt horse in the coach! Oh, awesome – you've brought the horses too!'

'Of course!' said Lucy, who was now sitting on the ramp sipping a glass of orange juice. 'Would we dream of having a summer holiday without our horses?!'

'True! I should have known – it would be totally not you.'

Alexa sat down beside her friend and offered Suzy a sip of her drink. 'Nowwww,' she said, 'you ready for the REALLY BIG SURPRISE?'

'What? Whaatt!'

'Liqui, Hope, Lucy and me will beeee . . .'

'What!' Suzy was jumping up and down on the spot. 'What? Tell me now, brat!'

'ON THE ROUND-UP with you and Ripple!' shrieked Alexa.

'For real?' asked Suzy in disbelief.

'Yes, for real!'

'Awesome, how utterly and totally awesome!' Suzy shrieked joyfully.

She thought back to her conversation with Mike, and her comment about not much more being able to happen in one day. How wrong was that!

'Wow,' she said, 'I can't believe it! How —' She stopped suddenly. 'Oh gawd, I'd better get on with my chores. I'll catch you all later . . .'

She jumped off the side of the ramp, unable to keep the big grin off her face, and strutted over towards the other tents just as Sam and Bubbles arrived. 'Hey, Sam,' she greeted him, 'take Bubbles over to the coach. Dad, Joe, Dawn and the girls are here – plus the four-legged girls, Liqui and Hope!'

Sam looked slightly sheepish as he opened his rein to turn Bubbles. 'Ah, yeah . . . what a great surprise!'

'You already know!' Suzy said accusingly. 'You were in on it too, weren't you?'

'Well, kind of,' he grinned, 'but it was really the big cowboy's decision.'

He rode Bubbles over to the coach, where Alexa greeted him. 'Well, it's Sam the Man! Hi, Sam! Howdy partner, that's a mighty pretty horse you're riding!' she said, in a poor imitation of a southern cowboy's drawl. 'That'd be the prettiest horse I've eva seen, and a mighty handsome cowboy ridin' that there horse too!'

Sam laughed. He and Alexa had a kind of special connection, and he was well used to her outbursts by now.

'Hey, Sam!' said the more restrained Lucy. 'I see you've got some nice Western apparel too. And Bubbles is beautiful – good choice! You look really good up there, Sam.'

Sam rose up in the saddle, stuck out his chest and grinned broadly. 'Yeah, I think she's pretty cool all right. In fact, I already love her as much as Bess, and I've only known her a little while!'

He reached forward and put his arms around Bubbles' neck. Bubbles blinked her big brown eyes – she knew she had a special jockey on board, and she knew she belonged with Sam.

As the others came out to admire Bubbles, Sam felt proud of his horse – she was responding really well to all the attention she was receiving. 'Don't worry, she's not as cheeky as Ripple,' he said. 'She won't steal your hat or anything.'

'So where are you at with your riding, Sam?' Alexa asked. 'Flying changes? Cutting cattle? Jumping? Piaffe? Trick riding . . . ?'

'Yeah, right!' Sam laughed. 'Well, I *can* canter her in 20-metre circles, and do simple changes and rein backs, and um . . . lots of other stuff . . .' He reached down and proudly stroked her neck again. 'She's a very clever horse!'

Suddenly becoming serious, he announced, 'Well, I'd better get her back, I've got my duties to attend to.' Sam sounded as if he had worked on White Cloud Station for the past fifty years. 'I'm cooking tonight, too, and it's not fish!'

'But I love your fish, Sam,' Alexa replied, pretending to be disappointed. 'Seriously, though – I'm impressed, it hasn't taken you long to learn all those movements. We'll have you in the dressage arena in no time!'

'Do many boys do dressage?' Sam asked innocently. 'Or is it a girl's thing?'

'Oh no, there are lots of famous male dressage riders!'

'Oh yeah, there's the Spanish Riding School in Vienna, isn't there. Not quite the West Grove Riding School! Actually Mrs Stevenson showed me a cool book about it – boy, would I love to go and see the lipizamas one day.'

'They're Lipizzaners, Sam,' Alexa corrected him. 'Those white stallions – they're so amazing. I'd love to go there too. Did you know the riding hall there is about 300 years old, Sam?'

'Blimey, that's oldddd – even older than Grandad!' he laughed, then, mimicking his Uncle George, added, 'I'd love to hear more, but right now I've got my jobs to take care of.'

'Sure, Sam. Hey, I might even take you there one day, huh?'

'Cor, all the way to Austria? That's a mighty long way.'

He gathered up the reins and gently turned Bubbles, and they trotted back towards the barn.

'There goes one happy kid,' Alexa said, wiping

away a tear with the back of her hand. 'That Sam I Am, I Am a Horse Man!'

'He's a great kid!' Lucy agreed, giving a wave to Sam who was glancing back to see if they were still watching. 'You're right, that's one happy kid! And he's got all the right qualities to become a really good horseman too!'

'He has indeed!' a voice behind them announced. Startled, they turned as Grandad Phillips appeared out of nowhere. He added with a smile, 'There's great happiness to be found on the back of a horse!'

He seems happy, thought Suzy, who had finished her rounds of the tents and rejoined her friends; so much happier. There was a pause as they all watched Sam ride away, then Grandad Phillips continued '. . . No hour of life is lost that is spent in the saddle.'

He nodded at his audience: 'Winston Churchill. I'll see you good folk soon. Dinner's at six – doesn't do to keep my darling wife waiting,' he said, pointing his stick at the big house jokingly. He paused again, looking over towards Sam and Bubbles. 'Oh my goodness, yes, there's great happiness on the back of a horse.' And off he headed, with an ever-so-tiny spring in his bandy old legs.

Puzzled, Alexa looked at Suzy. 'I got the impression from what you said in your emails that Grandad Phillips was a bit . . . you know . . . grumpy. He seemed cheery enough?'

'Well,' Suzy replied thoughtfully. 'Perhaps that was my first impression, but some pretty huge things have happened around here lately.'

'Like what?'

'Well, for one, we came up with a plan to get Grandad riding again.'

'It's hard to imagine that old fella on a horse!' Alexa giggled.

'Imagination is a great thing,' Suzy said, mock seriously, 'because it was through our imaginations that we got Grandad Phillips riding again, on Ripple!'

After she had explained the events that led up to Grandad's ride Alexa piped up, 'By the way, *is* that your iPod hanging around his neck?'

'Was!' Suzy smiled.

21

Cowboys Cooking

There was quite a crowd gathered on the veranda and lawn at the side of the house. Mike and Sam were cranking up the coals of the barbecue, and things were smoking nicely. They were dressed for the occasion in their Western attire, Sam in his new wranglers, although because he hadn't quite grown into them yet they kept slipping down a bit.

Grandma was sitting at the top end of the trestle table, and Grandad was standing beside her overseeing the cooks. Grandma had her long hair pulled up into a swirly bun, and tonight she had red lipstick on. From her ears hung silver horseshoes with tiny turquoise stones; the same earrings as in the portrait, Suzy noticed. Grandad was dressed in an open-necked black, grey and turquoise checked shirt, and his jeans were held up by a thick leather belt with a large, shiny engraved buckle, similar to the one on his saddle.

The cowboys and other round-up riders had congregated to discuss the round-up, and Lucy and Alexa were there with Joe, Dawn, and Suzy's father, Andrew. There was fruit punch, beer, and sparkling apple juice set out on a side table, and an assortment of nibbles.

'Mmm,' mumbled Alexa, as the girls eyed up the array of delicious-looking food; 'I hope they have something suitable for a vegetarian palate!'

'Come on, help yourselves, girls,' Cynthia encouraged them. 'There are chippies, pâté, pesto dips. Make yourselves at home and eat up – enjoy!'

Suzy took some chips and dip then looked around at the strangers, who were all eating and laughing easily. She recognised the woman who had been riding the Arab at last year's round-up, and decided she would go over and chat to her and find out more about her horse. There was an atmosphere of camaraderie – after all, they were all there for the same reason – the horses. Stories were flying left, right and centre, and Suzy noticed that Lucy and Alexa were also in their element and mixing well. Lucy could sometimes be a bit shy, but there she was chatting away to a cowgirl about barrel racing. Alexa, meanwhile, was entertaining a group of cowboys by telling them about Bones, and their efforts to get him to stand up and not fall over under the weight of the driftwood. Suzy noticed how the different generations all got along together, one of a kind. Yes, she thought, this is great – we are one big equine family.

* * *

'Food's ready,' shouted one of the cowboys, who had joined Mike and Sam and was helping at the barbecue. 'Come and get it!'

The eager crowd headed toward the barbecue, where Sam and Mike were dishing out steaks, sausages and patties.

'Especially for you, Alexa, vegetarian patties,' laughed Mike as Alexa surveyed the food slightly hesitantly. 'Suzy told me you don't eat meat.'

'Yum, thanks,' Alexa replied, taking a couple of the patties.

Cynthia had provided a range of colourful salads, and they were disappearing fast as everyone filled their plates. Soon they had all found a place at the long table, and the talking died down a little as they concentrated on the delicious food.

Suzy noticed how Grandma and Grandad Phillips made a point of talking to just about everyone who was there, greeting them all and making sure they felt at home. Grandad looked very distinguished, and Grandma was the picture of elegance, graceful and poised – all those years of riding had helped her maintain her stylish posture, and she still sat beautifully upright.

After the cowboys had had a second round and the babble of voices started up again, Grandad stood up and clanged his spoon against the stem of his wine glass. 'Now,' he said firmly, 'before dessert, I've got a few words to say.'

The crowd hushed and turned to listen.

'Firstly, I'd like to welcome you all to the annual round-up at White Cloud Station. It's good to see familiar faces again, and there are also some new ones we need to welcome. Lucy, Alexa and Suzy – stand up please. These young ladies will be riding out with you experienced folk tomorrow – I know they'll be well looked after, but keep an eye on them, you know how these young 'uns can be,' he joshed. Then, looking at Suzy, he added with a smile, 'And watch out for that curly horse! He's liable to get up to all sorts of tricks!'

As the girls sat down, Grandad once more tapped his spoon against his glass. 'I'd also like to introduce you to a young man who is to receive a special mention for his bravery tonight. Sam, can you stand up please.'

Sam looked a bit bewildered as he quickly put his sausage down and wiped the sauce from around his mouth. He sucked in his lips and squinted, feeling slightly embarrassed about receiving another mention. After all, he had already appeared in the newspaper.

Grandad told the story of the incident at the cave, and how Sam had rescued Suzy and Ripple and led them to safety at Castle Point. There were a few gasps from the crowd, and murmurs about the initiative shown by someone so young, then they all burst into applause for the young hero.

Grandad shook Sam's hand and passed him his reward, a black leather belt almost identical to the one Grandad himself was wearing. It was engraved with his name and the initials 'WC'.

'Wow, amazing!' Sam grinned delightedly as he threaded the belt through the loops of his jeans, before adding hastily, 'Thanks, Grandad!'

'And while I have your attention, folks – Mike, come up here, son,' Grandad commanded. Mike went to stand beside his grandfather, who looked up at his much taller grandson and handed him an envelope.

'You'll need this when you go to Veterinary College next term,' he announced proudly. Then, looking round at the crowd, he continued, 'We're going to have a doctor in the family – a doctor for the horses!' He shook Mike's hand and nodded his approval.

'Thank you, Grandad.' They embraced, then Mike walked back to sit with the other cowboys and the crowd came alive with chatter again.

'One last thing!' Grandad interrupted. 'There's nothing like a horse to get an old man cranked up again! We'll have dancing later, but first, I have to pay tribute to a special horse that lifted my spirits and made me ride into life again. I may look old but at heart I'm just young like Sam here!'

Sam looked up, taking a moment from admiring the large, shiny silver buckle in front of his belly. Grandad tapped his shoulder affectionately and they both smiled.

Then, from the back of the crowd came Ron, leading Ripple. He took Ripple to the table, where Grandad was holding a black woollen rug. On the side in turquoise writing were the words 'WHITE CLOUD RIPPLE'. Suzy was stunned. She had always wanted a show rug, and with the events on the horizon it was perfect. Ron helped put the rug over Ripple's back and the horse bobbed his head up and down as if in appreciation of the honour.

'A toast to this very special horse,' Grandad announced.

'To White Cloud Ripple!' the crowd responded.

Suzy felt proud, not only of her horse, but of the way they had pulled together to make Grandad so happy. It was as if they had given the old man a new lease of life. So what if he's old, she thought. He's still a horseman, a horse rider, and he's brilliant at it!

'Oh, thank you, thank you, Grandad!' she said, getting up and going round to give him a hug. 'That's going to be his show name – "White Cloud Ripple" – you will be proud of us, Grandad, you wait and see.'

Suzy turned towards Ripple, and made as if to lead him away. Ron smiled as she approached. 'I'm happy to take him back for you, Suzy. You relax and enjoy your friends. It's not every year you get to have a fun evening like this. Ripple's used to me, eh Ripple? We'll put you back with your friends too.'

Ripple pawed the ground and everyone laughed. He looked at his audience, but was this display really for them or was he keen to get moving back to his grassy pasture?

22

The Stars

Dessert was delicious – Sam couldn't resist a second helping of the fresh fruit salad and apple crumble with cream. After the empty plates and the remains of the food had been cleared, the tables were stacked away and the crowd sat about casually on the outdoor furniture and some hay-bales that had been brought up from the barn. Grandad and Mike had organised a blues band, who set up in one corner with an area for dancing in front of them.

Grandad and Grandma Phillips led off the dancing, and the crowd fell silent as they watched the old couple intently. Grandad sang to his wife as they danced, and it would have been hard to find a dry eye in the audience. They were, after all, the reason White Cloud Station and the round-up of wild horses took place. The old couple seemed to have passed a magic of their own to White Cloud, and they were undoubtedly the stars of the evening.

Halfway through the song, others joined in the dancing. The girls got up and danced, and the music revved up as spirits became more lively. The place was on fire with fun, laughter and dancing. The moon was out and the stars were shining, sparkling their magic over the crowd and over White Cloud Station.

After a while Grandma decided she needed a rest, so after a good-night kiss from Grandad she was escorted inside by Cynthia and Ron. Grandad, taking advantage of his new lease of life, decided he would stay for another half-hour and then join her.

Suzy looked down over the campsite, thinking how lucky she was to be up here at the homestead and riding tomorrow – it's like a dream come true, she thought. Grandad was chatting happily, talking about one of his favourite topics – wild horses – and of course he had the ideal audience. The energy was exhilarating, for it resonated of horse. As Suzy commented to Alexa, 'This is like putting the Warmblood Quarter Horses, Arabs, Andalusian, brumbies, mustangs and Shetlands all together – they're all basically horses. These people are the same – we're all here because we are the same, we all share one thing in common – our love of horses. Like, how cool is this? We are all here for the horses!'

'Well,' Alexa replied, and Suzy could tell by her tone that she had made a mistake by confiding something so heartfelt to her, 'see that big, fat man over there, wearing braces because his tummy hangs over his belt, well he'd be your typical Clydie, and that woman, well, with a bum like hers I'd say she'd be a pure-bred quarter horse, now glance over that way, and . . .'

'Stop it, Alexa! You know what I mean! You are horrible sometimes!'

'Oops, sorry. I was just trying to be funny – I'll shut my big mouth! I, of course, am beautiful like my Liqui! But I tell you what . . .'

'What?'

'There's Koru the Great! See Grandad over there – he'd have to be the wisest and most knowing horse of all. That is, of course, if he was a horse – you know, what we were just talking about . . .' For once in her life Alexa was tongue-tied. 'I think I'd better shut up!'

Suzy glanced over at Grandad Phillips and

wondered what it must be like to be his age. She thought about all the stories about horses he must have to tell. I mean, she thought, that's an awful lot of time! I think I already know lots about horses, but what must he know?

Much as she loved her friend, Suzy wasn't in the mood for Alexa's frivolity. She was in a reflective mood. She felt that a period of her life had ended and a new part was beginning. Suddenly she felt more grown up, less of a child, even if sometimes she did feel like Goldilocks. There had been a change in her; there was now some really serious stuff in her life, like rounding up the wild horses, minding Sam, caring for Ripple, and competing and hopefully winning at national level. She had responsibilities and purpose.

* * *

It was getting late and the guests were starting to leave. The girls were sitting on a hay-bale together looking out over the horses, and the barn was lit up by the full moon.

'Why is it that when we get together on special occasions it seems the moon is always full?' Suzy asked.

'That's because we're special, and someone up there is organising the heavens just for us,' laughed Alexa. 'A full moon – well, that means it's an exciting and dynamic time for us. Well, not just us, for everyone.'

'You really believe in astrology, don't you Alexa?' Lucy asked seriously.

'Of course, it's for real,' Alexa said firmly. 'You can fish by it, garden by it. And ride by it too. Yep, it's all written in the stars!'

'I guess you're right,' Suzy replied. 'It's all going pretty well so far!'

'Yes,' replied Lucy, 'who would have thought—'

Alexa interrupted her: 'We're having the best-ever summer!'

Lucy joined in the chorus: 'A summer with horses! No one, just no one could wish for more!'

'C'mon,' Alexa laughed, 'we'd better get back to the camp-site, and you, oh snobby one, must retire to your boudoir!'

'Well, beats the tent! Ha ha! Jealous?'

'No, you're my friend. I don't get jealous of you any more,' Alexa said. She stood on the hay-bale as if to make a grand speech. 'I, Alexa Humble Pie, unconditionally love and accept that you, Suzy High Society, are not only a better rider and horsewoman, and prettier, but are also of a much higher class than us lower-ranking citizens of White Cloud Tent.'

'You're a clown sometimes, Alexa,' Lucy laughed. 'We mere mortals shall return out there into the wilderness and find a cave to sleep in. But fear not, for we shall be guided by the stars, we shall not fall or blunder along the way, and when morning does finally arrive may you send your servant to get us and we shall be reunited over a grand feast in preparation for the endless ride.'

They laughed, hugged, and said their good nights. Suzy walked, in her favourite old boots, towards the front door of the homestead. She stopped and glanced back at her friends, watching them as they walked towards the camping paddock. She smiled as she reflected on what a great summer she was having – the best she could remember in a long time.

The stones on the path crunched as she walked, breaking the silence of the still night. The moonlight lit the petals of Grandma's white roses and she paused to pick one. Its delicate scent reminded her of Rose Cottage and her mother's rose garden. Normally when she thought about her mother she felt sad, but tonight it felt different somehow.

It's because I'm surrounded by friends who understand me, she thought.

Her thoughts then turned to the coming round-up and before she knew it the butterflies had started.

Suddenly she thought of Ripple, and she knew he

would help to settle her nerves. It wasn't that the butterflies were scary, but they were making her restless, and she didn't know if she could get through the night with their excited fluttering. Ripple always soothed her, he always understood, and he was always there for her when she needed someone to listen. She crunched toward the barn, cringing slightly at the noise she was making on the path.

It seemed all of White Cloud was asleep, so she decided to jump over the garden and walk across the lawn. As she leapt over a rose bush her jeans caught and she tumbled to the ground, landing in a heap on the grass. She rolled onto her back and managed to free her jeans without ripping them too badly. She lay on her back and giggled, feeling warm and fuzzy inside. She sighed contentedly and looked up at the sky above, then she closed her eyes and imagined flying through the air on Ripple's back, riding into the mountains . . . amongst the wild horses.

Join the White Cloud Station Club

If you sign-up to this quarterly newsletter we will send you a White Cloud Station welcome pack with some fun goodies and the opportunity to win some great prizes.

We'll be the first to give you all the inside gossip from the girls of White Cloud Station and you can follow the fun adventures of Suzy, Alexa and Lucy.

Get your name in the White Cloud Station book!

Our first competition will be for one lucky reader to have their name featured as a character in the next White Cloud Station book. We may even want to take your photo!

Visit www.penguin.co.nz/whitecloud to sign up today!

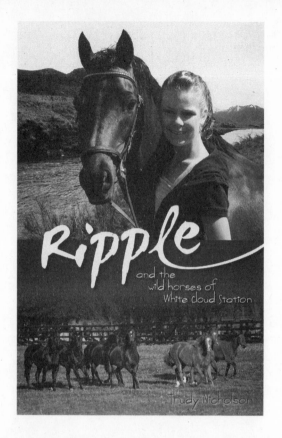

Book 1 in the White Cloud Station series.

Suzy, Alexa and Lucy live and breathe horses. But unfortunately for Suzy her allergies mean she is forbidden to have a horse of her own. When the three girls attend the round-up and auction of the wild horses at White Cloud Station, Suzy falls in love with a curly-coated horse that she desperately wants to buy. However, things don't go according to plan when he gets sold to another bidder.

Just when it looks like Suzy will never get her dream, an unexpected friend comes to the rescue.